"You," Leonie whispered as she stared at Guy

"They said they were keeping you in the hospital for the night."

"They tried to tell me that, too," he said. "But I had the queer idea that you'd take the opportunity to run away. It seems I wasn't wrong." He looked her over contemptuously, his eyes on the suitcase in her hand.

She licked her lips. "I'm not running away," she said with difficulty, "I'm putting an end to something that was misguided and foolish in the first place. For which I take full responsibility . . . and this seemed to be the best way to do it."

"Then you left it too late," he said softly but with his eyes glittering. "Much too late, my dear. I want you, Leonie. And I'm going to have you. . . ."

LINDSAY ARMSTRONG was working for Lufthansa Airlines when she met and married an accountant from New Zealand. They decided to settle—if you can call it that—in Australia. Early on they blithely embarked on an epic camping trip, which carried them from coast to coast with four children. Then they moved on to a six-hundred-acre mixed grain property, which they eventually abandoned to the mice, the leeches and the constant black flies. Undaunted, they purchased an untried trotter—"mainly because he had blue eyes"—and went on to win twenty-seven purses. Now they've opted for a more conventional life in Brisbane, where Lindsay started to write and continued raising their five children. But when Lindsay looks to the future, she doesn't imagine for one moment they will stay put forever.

Books by Lindsay Armstrong

HARLEQUIN PRESENTS
559—MELT A FROZEN HEART
607—ENTER MY JUNGLE
806—SAVED FROM SIN
871—FINDING OUT

HARLEQUIN ROMANCE
2443—SPITFIRE
2497—MY DEAR INNOCENT
2582—PERHAPS LOVE
2653—DON'T CALL IT LOVE

These books may be available at your local bookseller.

Don't miss any of our special offers. Write to us at the following address for information on our newest releases.

Harlequin Reader Service
901 Fuhrmann Blvd., P.O. Box 1397, Buffalo, NY 14240
Canadian address: P.O. Box 2800, Postal Station A,
5170 Yonge St., Willowdale, Ont. M2N 6J3

LINDSAY ARMSTRONG

love me not

Harlequin Books

TORONTO • NEW YORK • LONDON
AMSTERDAM • PARIS • SYDNEY • HAMBURG
STOCKHOLM • ATHENS • TOKYO • MILAN

Harlequin Presents first edition June 1986
ISBN 0-373-10887-7

Original hardcover edition published in 1985
by Mills & Boon Limited

CHAPTER ONE

THE Runaway Bay marina lay quiet and slumbering in the white heat of a weekday, mid-summer high noon. No breeze stirred the rigging of any of the millions of dollars' worth of mostly luxury craft moored cheek by jowl to its piers, or fluttered any of the canvas awnings. No activity was taking place on the launching ramp or in the high, open-sided steel structure where smaller boats were stored like boxes in a shoe store but with the aid of a hydraulic lift. And there seemed to be no-one about gazing into the marina shops or taking a late, late breakfast of eggs Benedict at the restaurant.

There was, however, a silver Rolls Royce parked opposite the entrance gate to one of the piers—one of the few cars in the parking bays.

Leonie Powell stared at it as she idly waved her straw hat to and fro to dissipate the almost overpowering heat coming up from the concrete beneath her feet. Then she walked towards it and past it and through the open, steel-mesh gate that at night time had to be operated with a key card, opposite it.

The *Marie-Claire* was berthed at the end of the pier and all fifty foot of her gleamed a blinding white with just a narrow silver line edging her deck and square portholes. The only other colour about her was the dark blue of the canvas that shaded her high fly bridge and the back deck.

Leonie stopped and when she could discern no

sign of life, she called out, 'Mr Richardson? Could I have a word with you?'

There was no immediate reply so she waited a minute or so then rapped her knuckles on the fibreglass moulding of the back deck. 'Mr Richardson?' she called again, and shaded her eyes so that she could peer through the doorway that led into a cabin. But the light was so bright outside, even with sun-glasses she couldn't see much. Then the boat moved slightly and a tall figure appeared in the doorway and Guy Richardson said unpleasantly, 'Who the hell are you?'

Leonie smiled gently. He looked as if he'd been asleep. His dark hair was ruffled and awry—in fact from the dark shadows on his jaw line, he looked as if he might still have been asleep from the night before although he was wearing a pair of crumpled blue jeans. That's all he was wearing.

'I'm Leonie Powell, Mr Richardson,' she said and waited.

Guy Richardson looked her over thoroughly. She was a fairly tall woman with long, straight hair the colour of polished teak and disconcertingly grey eyes that sometimes seemed to capture the light. People often looked and looked again at her eyes once she looked at them fully, not only because they were lovely but also because she had a habit of looking down a lot, almost as if she was well aware of the riveting power of her eyes and despised it.

But today they were covered by a pair of large sun-glasses. Not a great deal of the rest of her was covered, though. All she wore was a sarong-type bikini top that looked as if it tied between her breasts but had a cunning little clasp hidden there.

It was a two-toned top, one side in a deep amethyst, the other in a pale, icy green. And beneath this wisp of silk she wore a pair of brief white shorts over the bikini bottoms, also two-toned in amethyst and green.

Which meant there was not a lot of her figure left to the imagination and Guy Richardson let no part of it go unstudied. From her slender, golden shoulders, to her breasts which were firm and rounded and needed no support, to the slimness of her waist, the curve of her hips and her long legs.

And she accepted his scrutiny unflinchingly as if she was perfectly relaxed—indeed, she returned it. From his broad shoulders to his taut diaphragm down to his bare feet. They both looked up at the same time but it was he who spoke.

'So?' he said without a flicker of recognition in his eyes. 'What's that supposed to tell me?'

'That was by way of introduction, Mr Richardson,' she murmured and smiled coolly, 'We've never met.'

He smiled himself then with some irony. 'I'm relieved to hear you say so. I'd be tempted to believe I'd gone senile if I thought I'd met you and forgotten you, Miss . . . Powell.'

'Leonie,' she corrected. 'I rang your office this morning. They told me you'd be here.'

'I see.' In a mystified way.

'Well, I came to ask a favour of you. Not . . . altogether a favour although it might seem so at first. You see, I'm a . . .' she hesitated, 'contributor to a national weekly women's magazine. And I thought an article on you and your new boat would make—great copy.'

'Did you now,' he replied. 'I must confess I

thought we'd both been done to death—I and my new boat.'

'You have, locally. You've made great copy. In Queensland. And possibly in all the trade magazines—boating magazines in other words.'

'Ah! I always wondered what that term meant!'

Leonie grimaced. 'I'm sorry. That was patronising.'

'Don't apologise. You were going well.' He lifted one dark eyebrow quizzically at her. 'It's just that I don't quite understand how it would advantage me to be featured in a national, weekly . . .'

'Women's magazine?' she interupted drily. 'You don't believe me, do you?'

'Miss Powell—Leonie if you prefer, due to certain circumstances beyond my control, I quite frequently find myself the target of . . . people who misrepresent themselves or request favours of me that aren't really favours.'

'I wasn't planning to do that, Mr Richardson,' she said steadily. 'I did have a certain *quid pro quo* in mind but that's up to you . . . In the meantime if I could present my credentials to you . . . um . . .?' She looked at him with her own eyebrows raised. 'Here on the jetty if you *like*.'

'Take your glasses off, Leonie,' he said abruptly.

Her knuckles showed white briefly on the basket she was carrying. Then she lifted her other hand and removed her sun-glasses and tucked them carefully into the basket before she raised her grey eyes and squinted. 'It's very bright, you know.'

'Come aboard then,' he said after a slight pause.

'Thank you.' She accepted his hand and climbed lightly over the back of the boat.

'And out of the sun,' he added and ushered her

into a large cabin that was pleasantly cool and
dim. It was a multi-purpose cabin, she discerned as
her eyes adjusted. A streamlined galley panelled in
what looked like walnut was fitted beneath large,
angled windows which would, when unshuttered,
look on to the forward deck, she guessed. The rest
of the area was uncluttered with built-in, comfortable settees round the walls, upholstered in
royal blue crushed velvet that was the same colour
as the close-pile carpet. Little tables were fitted
crosswise into the settees at intervals and the only
free standing piece of furniture in the cabin was a
round walnut table with a central pedestal leg,
beautifully carved, that she'd have given her eye
teeth to own.

He pulled the sliding door closed behind him.

Leonie looked up and down again almost
immediately.

'Only to keep the air-conditioning in,' he
drawled.

'It is cool in here,' she agreed. 'Well, Mr
Richardson.' She reached into her basket and
withdrew a magazine and flicked through until she
came to a two-page spread. Then she laid it on the
walnut table. 'This . . . is one of my articles. It was
published last year. It's about Moreton Island.'

He'd been leaning back against the door with
his arms folded across his chest, watching her.
After a moment he straightened and came forward
to study the magazine leaning on the table with
both hands. 'Mmm,' he said finally as he scanned
the by-line which undoubtedly said Leonie Powell
but if that wasn't proof enough, there was also a
picture of her standing on the beach at
Tangalooma—one of the six pictures that
accompanied the article. 'I see you're a crusader

against sand-mining on Moreton Island—as a matter of fact I agree with you.'

'You know . . . Moreton Island?'

'Very well. It's very beautiful and unspoilt. It would be a pity for it not to remain that way. A lot of Brisbane people—well, South Eastern Queenslanders get great pleasure from it. Uh . . . I notice you didn't bring your photographer with you.'

Leonie reached once more into her basket and withdrew an expensive and complicated looking camera. 'I do my own photography. It's a hobby of mine.'

He lifted an eyebrow at her and murmured, 'A lady of talent. Who took the one of you?'

'A kid I met on the beach. It was a miracle it turned out so well—or at all for that matter. He got quite excited and began to wave the camera around and all but dropped it in the water. As a matter of fact that's him.' She leant forward and pointed to another of the pictures, this time taken seaward with a smallish, freckled faced boy frolicking in the shallows. 'I got his address and when the magazine came out, I sent him a copy. His mother, who must have had a sense of humour, wrote back and said fame obviously does queer things to people—he spent all his pocket money buying up as many copies as he could afford, then he cut the articles out and autographed them and sold them to his mates.'

A faint grin touched Guy Richardson's lips. 'I wonder if he made a profit?'

She grinned back. 'I doubt it.'

'You have extraordinary eyes, Leonie,' Guy Richardson said quietly. 'Why didn't you want me to see them?'

Leonie drew back. 'What makes you think that?' she said casually. 'I couldn't very well have worn my sun-glasses in here.'

He shrugged. 'I guess not ... I just seemed to get that impression. Would you like something to drink?'

'Then ...' she hesitated. 'Am I in?' she asked whimsically.

'Let's just say,' he conceded with a glimmer of a smile, 'you've made it to first base.' He moved away from the table and opened a walnut cabinet that proved to be a fridge. 'What will it be? Champagne?'

'I ... coke, I think. Champagne does strange things to me in the middle of the day.'

'That could be interesting ...' He poured her a coke and opened a can of beer for himself. 'Sit down, Leonie,' he said and handed her the glass. 'And tell me what kind of strange things champagne does to you—in the middle of the day.' He sat down himself but not close to her.

The corners of her mouth twitched. But she said perfectly gravely, 'It sends me to sleep, I'm afraid.'

He laughed and she thought he looked younger suddenly, than she knew he was. Thirty-seven to be precise and his birthday was in May... She studied his face candidly as she sipped her coke and he his beer. And decided that his photos didn't say it all. Not even the colour ones. His eyes were not brown but a very dark blue although his tall well-built body gave no lie to his photos. It was his face in fact that differed most. In the flesh it was a more interesting face. Not handsome precisely but strong and it reflected the personality of a man who had seen a lot, done a lot—among other things, made himself a fortune out of boat designing and building. He also looked as if he'd had considerable experience with women—it was like an indefinable stamp on him. Just as you knew without being told that he'd be a tough business man, you also knew that he would attract a lot of women. It was an aura of strength and ruggedness but tempered by a finer edge somehow. Perhaps a sense of humour? Leonie reflected. But whatever, something that was obviously very hard to resist. Well, that's why I'm here, isn't it? she thought.

'You're very cool, my dear,' he said suddenly, when she at last looked away.

A fleeting smile touched her lips. 'I'm not a child, Mr Richardson.'

He was silent for a time. Then he said, 'All right, that being so, let's get down to business. This proposition of yours—what's in it for me?'

'It would be a good advertisement for your boat, this,' she gestured, 'being a prototype of a new design.'

'I don't generally sell my boats to women and children. The major subscribers, I should imagine, to your magazine.'

'Perhaps I should explain, it's not my magazine. They don't employ me. I freelance . . .'

'You must freelance very well if it supports you,' he interupted.

'Oh, it's not my main source of income,' she murmured.

'And what is?' He looked at her directly and she got the impression that she'd annoyed him. All to the good, Leonie. Isn't that what advertising is all about? Getting under the skin? And why should it be any different if it's yourself you're . . . pushing?

'That's my business, Mr Richardson,' she said.

'But shortly to become mine, I gather.' He leaned his head back and drained his beer. And when he looked back at her, there was a hard light in his blue eyes. 'Go on,' he said abruptly.

'Well, to get back to your point about women and ... particularly women, I disagree with you. Women may not buy your boats but they have the power of influence. And many women, reading the kind of article I had in mind, would associate your boats with you ... and the kind of glamour you exude. It would not be an uncommon phenomenon for them to then steer their boat-loving husband towards a Richardson designed and built craft, would it?'

'Are you asking me if I share your low opinion of women, Leonie?' he enquired with a shadow of a smile that didn't reach his eyes.

'I don't suppose women are the only ones who like to dream a little,' she said wryly, looking directly into his eyes.

And it was a long, merciless gaze he subjected her to but she didn't flinch.

Then he said. 'These boats come at a figure around three-hundred-thousand dollars, Leonie. Dreaming about them is the most a whole lot of people can do ...'

'But they're not the only boats you build, are they?' she countered softly. 'There are smaller, cheaper ones. We could mention that, too.'

'You've done your homework,' he remarked. 'And you put forward quite an interesting theory. But my boats are selling well enough as it is. Besides, what you've said *is* only theory. And I'm afraid, not enough inducement for me.'

'That wasn't all I had to bargain with.'

The silence stretched.

'You ... either rate yourself highly, my dear—I presume that's what you are offering? Correct me if I'm wrong?'

'No ...'

His mouth hardened. 'I thought not ...'

'If you consider that I'm rating myself very highly, Mr Richardson,' she said quietly and evenly, 'does that imply that you have an even higher opinion of *your*self that puts you way, way above me? I wonder what the difference is. Do you breath clearer, purer air?'

'I don't go around offering myself for sale, *Miss* Powell,' he said through his teeth.

'I think there'd be more to it than that. Nor was it a sale I had in mind. I thought more of a two-way thing ...'

'Your body for ...'

'I never use my body indiscriminately, Mr Richardson.' She looked at him steadily. 'Nor do I offer it ... lightly. But if you prefer to terminate this discussion—that's up to you.' She stood up and reached for her camera.

'If,' he said, 'offering one's body for the sake of a magazine article is not ... light, I don't now what is. I think I might have preferred it if you'd stuck a big label on your ... undeniably beautiful body, Leonie, with a dollars and cents sign on it.'

'Ah, but you see, dollars and cents are not quite all I have in mind. An article like this could be a big scoop for me. You have never really gone in for personal publicity, have you? Yet from a distance, you're quite a well-known figure. Apart from your boating exploits, racing exploits, there's that rescue you figured in so prominently on the Southport Bar. But I thought if I could slant this a little more personally ...'

'It would make great copy,' he said with a cynical twist to his lips. 'How personal did you intend to go? What I'm like in bed?'

She smiled faintly. 'Oh no. I'm not the kind of person who would sleep and tell. Besides, I think you may have got the wrong idea about that. My idea of . . . being with a man doesn't revolve solely around sex. I prefer it to be an exchange of ideas, a stimulation of each other's minds too.' She shrugged. 'Going to bed without that is rather pointless I've always thought. However, you might not agree.' She looked at him enquiringly.

But he said, 'Am I to take it that you foresee a . . . more stable career, perhaps of full-time journalism, if you get this scoop?'

'Ah. Now you're beginning to understand, Mr Richardson,' she said.

'I wonder. I've met not a few . . . fortune huntresses in my time, Leonie. They often have a good tale to spin. In fact it's like a stock in trade, you could say.'

'I could also say, the last thing I'm interested in is your fortune, Mr . . .'

'For God's sake call me Guy,' he interrupted irritably.

'Guy then,' she murmured. 'But I don't suppose you'd believe me.'

'No, I wouldn't.'

'But *would* you agree you're not some innocent young man easily to be taken for a ride?'

They stared at each other, he with his lips compressed into a white line, she perfectly relaxed and serene.

Then all of a sudden he was laughing. 'My God, Leonie, he said finally, 'you're clever—one might say almost diabolically clever. But,' he sobered and his dark blue eyes narrowed, 'there's still something I don't quite get about you . . .'

'I can tell you what that is,' she said calmly and reached for the magazine to tuck it into her basket. 'A lot of women—that I've observed anyway—feel they need to be coy about what they want from men, and that to be any other way is fast and forward and above all brazen. I don't. I think it's more honest in fact. But I'm afraid a lot of men also subscribe to the . . . brazen theory.'

'And I'm one of them?'

She shrugged delicately and slipped her sunglasses on. 'That remains to be seen.'

'All right,' he said, suddenly decisive and he stood up and surprised her by reaching out and removing her sun-glasses. 'We'll do it. With one proviso, Miss Powell,' he said and took her chin in one hand and stared down into her widened grey eyes that she tried to lower but he wouldn't release her chin. 'One proviso, that you don't try to hide your beautiful eyes from me. You have a trick of doing that I've noticed. Is *that* being coy or is it that they give away more than you like to?'

The only sign that Leonie was not as calm and serene as she had been minutes earlier was a faint fluttering of the delicate skin in the hollow at the base of her throat that she wasn't aware of, except to realise that he had noticed something that was giving her away, betraying some nerves. Because his eyes had narrowed again, probingly.

'It's . . . mostly an unconscious thing,' she said.

'Even unconscious things have their roots somewhere.'

'Then I'll dig into my . . . subconscious and see what I can come up with.'

'Do that, Leonie,' he murmured. 'In the

meantime, should we seal our bargain with a kiss? It might be appropriate.'

'We haven't made a bargain yet. I mean, we've made no arrangements . . .'

'Then, let's see . . . the school holidays begin in about ten days' time. I don't particularly want to be away before that. How would it be,' he looked over the top of her head thoughtfully, then back into her still captured face, 'if we took off for a week's cruising around the islands from the day after school breaks up? Would that . . . interfere with your schedule, Leonie?' His eyes were quizzically mocking.

'Actually it would suit me very well,' she said then grimaced slightly.

He released her chin. 'What was that for?'

'For . . . oh, you were hurting my chin.' She rubbed it lightly.

'You just did it again. Looked down.'

She swallowed and hoped he didn't notice that. In fact, she thought, he's more perceptive than I gave him credit for. And perhaps I've achieved enough for today anyway. What do they say? Get out while the going's good . . .

She held out her hand. 'We have a bargain now, Mr . . . Guy,' she said gravely. 'What time of day would you like to leave?'

'Nine o'clock in the morning. It doesn't much matter to me. I gather,' he looked at her amusedly, 'you don't believe in kissing to seal a bargain?'

'No,' she answered coolly. 'I believe in kissing for much better reasons.' She dropped her hand. 'But if you don't want to shake my hand, I don't mind. You have my word.'

'For what? That might be the big question.' He raised his eyebrows.

'That my camera and I will be here at nine o'clock in the morning on the day after school breaks up. I'll get in touch with you if anything unexpected crops up.' She pushed her glasses back on and turned towards the door.

'What happens if anything crops up un-expectedly for me?' he queried wryly.

She hesitated. 'Well, I'm not on the 'phone,' she said then her lips quirked. 'Why don't you put a personal ad. in the *Gold Coast Bulletin?*' she suggested.

'What should I say?'

'How about . . . Leonie, I've decided you're a gold-digger after all—signed, Guy. I'd understand that . . .'

He laughed. 'So long as we understand each other . . . All right, until then I bid you good-day, Miss Powell,' he said a shade drily and pushed open the door.

Hours later she swam up from a deep, deep sleep.

It was dark outside and she took a shower and slipped on her old Chinese silk kimono and made herself something to eat which she took out on to the back verandah.

One of the few advantages of her flat in an ancient weatherboard house that had been divided into three flats, was the view of Surfer's Paradise she got from this veranda.

The house occupied one of the higher points of Southport and her co-tenants, an elderly gentleman with an equally elderly dog and a much younger gentleman with an odd taste in clothes who kept very much to himself, were united in only one common cause. To frequently bemoan the way the landlord increased the rents

quarterly but appeared to have an inbuilt dislike
of effecting any repairs.

That it was not a glamorous place to live, no-one
could deny, but despite the rent increases it was
cheap compared to the units in the skyscrapers of
Surfer's Paradise, which was a consideration with
Leonie. In fact, she could have afforded better on
her salary but she preferred to save as much as she
could.

And, too, as she'd discovered, familiarity could
breed a sense of security and this had come in
several ways. 'Spider' Jones, the elderly man with
the dog would have been horrified to be thought
of as an 'old woman' but he'd taken a liking to
Leonie and was as comfortable to be with as a
fussy old lady. He worried about her, gave her
racing tips which she never backed and tirelessly
looked after what was supposed to be her section
of the garden. He also took great pains to
protect her from the queerness of Mr Hallsy, the
third tenant, although they all knew, Leonie as
well, that she was really quite safe from Mr
Hallsy.

Other things seemed to give her a sense of
security, too. It was an ugly old house and her flat,
which she rented furnished, was not precisely a
decorator's dream. But there was one white wall
down the drive where a red poinsettia grew with
tropical abandon that was quite breathtakingly
beautiful. And the back lawn, carefully tended and
mowed by Spider, was a lush green carpet that
stretched from the house to beneath a giant old
jacaranda tree and somehow, in its richness,
defeated the neighbouring yards and the stringy
fences between.

I could be worse off, she thought as she toyed

with her toasted cheese and finally whistled for Spider's dog who loved cheese.

I really could, she told herself as she listened to the dog crunching into the toast below the veranda. On the other hand, I haven't got a great deal to lose. My job possibly, but it's only a job ... Which is why I set myself this goal, isn't it? So why torture yourself because that goal is within a hand's grasp now, Leonie? Are you afraid? You shouldn't be, not you of all people ...

She sighed suddenly and answered herself honestly, 'I don't know. And I don't know why I feel so tired. As if I've been climbing Everest ... Conscience, perhaps? Well that's the last thing I should be suffering from ...'

CHAPTER TWO

'MISS Powell! Miss Powell, where were you yesterday? I missed out on my lesson. It's the only lesson I enjoy all week,' Claire Richardson said with a grin and a rolling of her eyeballs.

'I took the day off.'

'Weren't you well?'

'No . . .'

'I'm sorry. Feeling better?'

'Yes . . . Did you practise?'

'Well, I . . . no,' Claire Richardson confessed with a grimace. She was an enchanting twelve-year-old with long brown hair and velvety brown eyes that she must have inherited from her mother, Leonie thought. 'Oh, Powie, it's so close to holiday time and I'm so excited! My fingers just won't do what my brain tells them! That's the problem. I guess I just don't have what it takes to be another Wolfgang Amadeus,' she declared.

'I'm not asking you to be that,' Leonie said with a grin. 'But your Royal College of Music exams come up within a few short months, and I don't suppose you'll be doing much on your holiday, Miss Richardson. And your father would be very disappointed if you fail these ones. So I'm told.'

'I suppose Miss Lucas told you that,' Claire said knowledgeably and wearily. 'She always gets in a terrible flutter about Daddy.'

'Daddy pays the bills,' Leonie murmured.

'Claire shot her a probing glance. 'That's true,' she conceded. 'But I don't think even he expects you to *manufacture* a child prodigy. I mean, we all know I'm no budding Eileen Joyce, Daddy, too. If anyone is that, it's you. You give me the goose bumps when you play.'

Leonie was silent for a time. Then she smiled. 'Thank you, Claire. But I'm not a budding Eileen Joyce, either. So you're looking forward to your holiday? I'm not surprised. But won't you miss your father?'

'I always miss my father a little bit,' Claire said wryly. 'But last time I went over to visit my grandparents in France, he came, too, and I think it made him a little bit sad. It reminded him of Mummy ... I was too young when she died to remember her. And anyway, he said this time they could have me all to themselves! I do spend all my other holidays with him. And,' she said, her dark eyes glowing, 'he's got special permission to take me out for the week-end on his new boat!'

'That sounds super,' Leonie murmured. 'All right,' she added, 'I'll forgive you for not practising this once. So long as you don't make a habit of it.'

'You're a honey, Miss Powell!' Claire said enthusiastically and danced away to go into her English class. No doubt to twist her English teacher round her little finger, Leonie reflected. For it was a well-known fact within the hallowed portals of St Bede's School for girls, one of the most select private schools in the state, that Claire Richardson was an expert at it. Even Miss Lucas, the senior music teacher and Leonie's immediate superior, who was a dour-faced spinster of fifty, had been heard to remark that she couldn't resist the child.

But as Leonie walked on towards the music

block, she suffered a slight qualm. It had been obvious yesterday that the name of Leonie Powell had not meant anything to Guy Richardson. Yet what if Claire mentioned it this week-end? Well, for one thing, she assured herself, no-one here knows me as Leonie—if any of the girls have discovered my first name which they seem to delight in doing—they'll find it's Helen ... And for another, Powell is a fairly common surname and *finally*, what could there be to suggest a link between the Leonie Powell of yesterday and Miss Powell, second-string music teacher at St Bede's? I've not been in any school photos so far ... No, and even if she were to describe me, she's only ever seen me with my hair in a bun and the rather dowdy clothes that are considered good taste here. No, I should be quite safe. Of course, he's going to have to know one day, but if I play my cards right, he mightn't care then ...

'If I play my cards right,' she echoed beneath her breath with a sudden shiver. 'He wasn't ... quite what I expected. Better or worse? Cleverer, perhaps. But all the same he fell for it, so ...'

'There you are, Helen!' Miss Lucas said, coming unexpectedly out of one of the music cubicles. 'Sorry to hear you were ill yesterday but it was no great loss! Oh, by that I mean with the holidays so near it's almost a waste of time being here. No-one's interested in being taught music at the moment! Her rather booming voice was tinged with bitterness. For music was Miss Lucas's life.

'I know what you mean,' Leonie murmured.

'But what with the musical coming up and the exams,' Miss Lucas continued bitterly, 'it's simply not good enough! By the way, I've just consulted with the head and it's to be the *Pirates of*

Penzance, one of her favourites,' she added gloomily.

Leonie smiled slightly because she now knew Miss Lucas well enough to know that Gilbert and Sullivan was not her cup of tea. But she said, although a little diffidently 'If we could persuade the girls to ... look upon it as a fun project, you know, dressing up as boys and so on, we at least might have their enthusiasm.'

Miss Lucas deliberated then brightened fractionally. 'That's a thought. Have you had much experience producing musicals, my dear Helen?'

'No,' Leonie said cautiously, 'but I rather enjoy them.'

'Then you're a godsend!' Miss Lucas pronounced. 'Because I must say you have a way with the girls, too, I've noticed. Come into my office and let us discuss some ideas ...'

Two days later, Leonie encountered the headmistress, Miss Carter, who stopped her and said, 'Miss Powell, Miss Lucas has been telling me some of your ideas for the musical. I thought they sounded very original. Miss Lucas is,' the head's lips twitched, 'looking a little less hag-ridden about the whole business, too. Thanks to you.'

Leonie looked uncomfortable but in fact couldn't help feeling warm inside, and gratified. Because in her months at St Bede's, she'd come to admire Miss Carter quite considerably. She was a tall woman but she carried herself well and with the kind of dignity that automatically commanded respect. Yet Leonie had learnt that she was a practical person, too, particularly when it came to dealing with girls. She had not placed outmoded restrictions on them which did not mean to say she could not, when necessary, be quite frighteningly stern.

'All young things need discipline sometimes,' she'd said once in Leonie's hearing, 'also a routine.'

But while she believed in keeping her charges busy even out of school hours, it was in a constructively creative way, and often, fun.

She also placed great emphasis in the whole conduct of the school, on truthfulness and what she termed, moral fortitude.

What on earth she would think of me and what I'm about to embark upon, Leonie reflected with a shiver, after that brief meeting, doesn't bear thinking about. But perhaps ... I wonder if they realise, the Miss Carters and Miss Lucases of this life, who've chosen this almost monastic life—Miss Lucas was a housemistress and lived at the school too—what kind of pressures you come up against out there in the world?

And I wonder if all their charges live up to the high standards they set here, once they've grown up and have left here, and they fell in love—or think they do?

'And who owns this boat you're going on, Leonie?' Spider asked with unabashed curiosity. It was break-up day, the evening of break-up day. Leonie had got home from school at about five o'clock, long after all the children had departed, particularly Claire Richardson who'd had a plane to catch to Sydney at nine o'clock in the morning to make her connection with a Paris flight. But even the music department of St Bede's needed to be wound down and she and Miss Lucas had worked at it all afternoon. Once home Leonie had changed into shorts and a T-shirt and was now sharing her after-dinner coffee with Spider Jones on the back veranda.

'Just a friend's, Spider,' she said.

Spider wrinkled his already wrinkled brow and gazed at her through his pebble thick glasses. 'Didn't think you had many friends, if you don't mind me saying so.'

Leonie smiled. 'I don't and I don't mind you saying so. But I've only been on the Coast for six months so . . .'

'True. Still and all, a pretty, young lass like your-self needs to get out and about.'

'Well that's just what I'm doing! For a whole week! And you don't have to worry about me, Spider. I'm going to have the time of my life.'

Spider was silent for a time, ruminating. Then he said, 'Boats can be dangerous things. Hope your friends know what they're doing. I've lived on the Coast all my life, and year in and year out people never learn!'

'I don't think . . .'

But Spider was away and running. 'Take the Southport Bar. I'd like to have a quid for the number of boats come to grief trying to cross it, I tell you! They just don't understand it's a tricky, treacherous crossing—all bars are! Take Jumpinpin. Look what happened to that fishing trawler a few months back when it was trying to come in. Now they were experienced but they copped it all the same . . .'

Leonie, who was sitting on the top step, leant her head back against the veranda wall and switched off, in a fashion. As a matter of fact she *was* thinking of the Southport Bar, that narrow strip of water between the Spit and the southern tip of South Stradbroke Island that was the marine

passage from the protected waters of the Southport
Broadwater, to the open sea. It didn't look
dangerous from land, although you could see the
surf between the long sandy finger of the Spit and
the scantily vegetated point of Stradbroke. But
from way across the Broadwater, which really was
an almost land-locked estuary of the Nerang
River, it never looked too fiercesome. Perhaps the
Broadwater itself fooled you, she thought and
visualised how beautiful it could be dancing with
sunlight in the early mornings, a fabulous
shimmering aquamarine sometimes.

It was often busy too, especially on week-ends,
busy with cruise boats that plied the routes
between the mainland and the dozens of islands
that formed a natural barrier from the open sea,
from Southport right up to Moreton Bay into
which the Brisbane River emptied. Busy with
speed boats, week-end fishermen, cabin cruisers,
catamarans, yachts, dinghies. Then there were the
bathers who favoured its more protected waters to
the surf of Main Beach, just on the other side of
the Spit, and Narrowneck, and Surfer's Paradise
itself, only a stone's throw virtually, from the
southern end of the Broadwater. There was
Fisherman's Wharf too, a new complex where you
could eat and drink and shop and buy fresh fish
and prawns straight from the trawlers that berthed
there, and there was Sea World ... it was a
fascinating and colourful place, the Broadwater.

But what I'm really wondering, Leonie mused,
is, will he go over the bar? I don't know if I'm
quite brave enough for that ...

She turned her head as Spider's words impinged
on her consciousness again.

'What was that?'

'I said don't forget to take some sun-tan lotion along, either. I know you've got quite a nice tan but you don't want to invite skin cancer, we have the highest rate of it in the world, so they say!'

Leonie chuckled quietly. 'What with dangerous bars, skin cancer, lunatics in boats—you've quite managed to frighten the life out of me, Spider!'

'Ah, well now,' Spider said, relenting a little, 'I really only want you to have a good time. You deserve it. But it's just as well to be warned. And don't worry, I'll look after your pot plants and make sure no-one burgles your flat—there's a hell of a lot of that going on too, y'know!'

But Leonie made her escape gracefully and affectionately.

And in the privacy of her flat, she set about packing. Not that she had a great deal to pack but most of it was new.

It had also been carefully chosen to create the right impression. Two new bikinis to begin with. They'd cost a small fortune but their cut and design were lovely and what's more the material and detailing showed they were expensive and not to be picked up at any of the dozens of beach-wear shops that abounded in Surfer's. No, these two were each originals. Then there was a sarong in a crinkly, semi-diaphanous polyester chiffon in muted shades of pink and grey and with gold threads running across it . . .

She tried it on over one of her new bikinis and decided that when it was wrapped round her body, while it did hide the details, it also outlined the shape quite dramatically. Then she tried it knotted around her waist instead of under her arms and found she could make a long skirt, or folded in half, a shorter skirt, each with a tantalizing slit up her thigh.

She took it off and folded it carefully and reached for the two blouses she'd bought. Both looked and felt like silk but again were a polyester mix. One was in a lovely dusky pink, the other a pale, powder blue and she thought that with their long sleeves but almost filmy texture they'd be ideal cover-ups when she'd had enough sun. She tried the pink one on, again over a new bikini, this time the mulberry one, and rolled the sleeves up to half-way between her wrists and elbows and tied the fronts into a knot at her midriff—and grimaced at her reflection in the mirror. She could have stepped right out of the society pages of a magazine, provided society had been boating or swimming.

Well, that's what I wanted to achieve, she mused, as she took the pink blouse off.

There was one more item that she tried on. A white dress in an uncrushable crêpe. It moulded her figure perfectly and the halter neckline showed off her tanned shoulders. In fact the white altogether looked good against her carefully acquired and nurtured tan. And to go with it were a pair of high-heeled gold kid mules. She pulled a slight face as she tried on the mules. They were very high and she wished she'd had time to break them in a little, or at least get used to them.

'Then again,' she murmured to herself, 'I might not get to wear this outfit. Who knows? Right, enough parading, Leonie. Let's get packed.'

As well as her new clothes, a couple of pairs of shorts and T-shirts went into the bag, a pair of jeans and a navy-blue sloppy-joe type sweater, a pair of sand-shoes, a short, terry towelling robe in gorgeous Maratea Lilac, some lacy underwear and a grey silk nightgown. Into a smaller bag went shampoo and conditioner, a wildly expensive body lotion and a small cut-glass phial of perfume and a bare minimum of make-up. That was it, she decided and looked around. The shorts and T-shirt and sandals she planned to wear tomorrow were laid out, her sun-hat on the table—she reached over for two paperbacks she'd bought and pushed them into the bag. What was left . . . of course! Her camera! How could she have forgotten that!

Take hold, Leonie, she admonished herself as she re-packed the blue canvas bag with camera and film at the bottom. Take hold . . . She also put in her savings bank book as an afterthought.

But when she woke at about three o'clock in the morning after sleeping restlessly, she didn't try to go back to sleep. Instead she got up and made herself a cup of tea and decided this was one night she was going to have to sweat it out, awake . . .

The weather had held.

In fact the dawn had been a symphony of colour as the sun rose into a clear sky but as Leonie caught the eight-fifteen bus for Paradise Point which stopped off at Runaway Bay, in the centre of busy Southport, the sky was only blue, a limitless blue with no sign of cloud.

And all she could think of as the bus lumbered through the back streets of Southport, was that Guy Richardson would most probably have reneged, although there had been no personal ad. in the *Gold Coast Bulletin* . . .

If he has, I'll just catch the next bus home, she told herself. End of chapter and verse and bad luck . . .

But at the same time she couldn't deny a stirring of fear at the pit of her stomach which refused to be quelled—the kind of shaky feeling you experienced about going to the dentist. Nor could she hide from herself that beneath her bravado, she was insidiously hoping that he had reneged.

Yet there were other things, she knew, that would keep her going on this course she'd set for herself. If he was there, she would go . . .

He was there, apparently waiting for her, standing on the pier leaning negligently against an electricity dispenser and he didn't stir when she stepped on to the pier but watched her walk towards him all the way down . . .

Then, when she stopped in front of him and put down her bag and guitar case—her guitar had been another afterthought, he straightened and said mockingly, 'Another talent?'

She shrugged.

'Well, you're dead on time, anyway. But I must confess I thought you'd have second thoughts.' His voice was dry. He wore jeans again and a striped T-shirt and he looked to her big and formidable, and not in a very good mood.

'I thought the same of you,' she said quietly.

He raised his eyebrows. 'How did you come?'

'I got a lift . . .'

'And how did you propose to get home if I wasn't here?'

'A taxi, I guess.'

He studied her in silence for a time. Then he said, 'Don't you have *any* qualms about . . . taking on a strange man, on a boat of all places? Not the easiest place to escape from unless you're an Olympic swimmer in disguise.'

She lifted a hand and took off her sun-glasses. 'It's a risk you take with any man,' she said levelly. 'In your own home, in your own bedroom.'

They stared at each other.

'I see,' he said at last as if something had suddenly become clear to him. Then he bent down and picked up her bags and put them on board and vaulted himself over and held out a hand to her. 'Welcome aboard the *Marie-Claire*, Leonie,' he said easily.

She put her hand in his after a barely perceptible hesitation and climbed on board herself.

'This way, ma'am. You haven't seen the other cabins, have you? Down those stairs ...' He gestured for her to go ahead into the main cabin and down a short, narrow flight of stairs beside the galley. 'I went more for comfort down here than the number of bodies you could accommodate so there are only two cabins and the bathroom. That's mine,' he said from right behind her as they came abreast a door panelled in the same wood as the passageway, 'that's the bathroom, and that's yours ...'

She pushed open the door and gasped because in what was really a very small space, was an exquisite little bedroom fitted out with every luxury.

A bed, not a bunk, with room to walk round three sides of it, one wall completely panelled in mirrors, the opposite one with a built-in wardrobe and dressing-table complete with stool. And looking gorgeous against the same dark wood used everywhere, an apricot carpet that exactly matched the duvet cover and frilled pillow case and valance on the bed.

'It's lovely,' she said.

'It was done with a certain . . . person in mind,' he said, as if he'd being going to say something else.

Child? she wondered and could just picture Claire's vibrant dark curls and eyes in this setting.

'Will she mind . . .?' Leonie bit her lip.

'She won't know.' There was something abrupt in the way he said it. But he added normally. 'You're under the foredeck and these skylights wind up if you need air. See?' He demonstrated. 'They're like portholes on the roof. But when we're under way they should be closed.' He wound it down. 'Which we will be shortly, but you have time to unpack. I'll leave you to it. Come up when you're ready.'

Leonie sank down on to the bed and stared at the door he'd closed behind him and discovered she felt sick . . . and trapped. But I'm not trapped, she told herself. I can stay here of my own free will, or I can go now, before it's too late. Only what will that achieve? Another failure in a seemingly long line of failures. I vowed I'd do this, it's something I *have* to do . . .

She took a deep breath and stood up and began to unpack and stow her clothes in Claire Richardson's pretty little cabin.

When she'd finished she wandered upstairs to find the main cabin empty, and went out on to the back deck. At the same time, a muted roar started bneath her feet and the deck vibrated slightly and she looked upwards to see that Guy Richardson was up on the fly bridge at the controls. She hesitated briefly then started to climb up the ladder-like steps fixed to the wall, to join him.

'Crew reporting,' she said as she stepped on to

the fly deck. 'Only this particular crew member is a novice, I'm afraid.'

He turned his head and did the strangest thing. He held out his hand to her and smiled, not mockingly, just quite ordinarily and he said, 'I'd rather have a novice than someone who *thinks* they know it all. Right, see these things that look like handles? That's what I steer with. And getting out of the Runaway Bay marina is rather like getting out of a crowded supermarket parking lot, so what you can do for me is keep watch and tell me if I'm about to crunch the boat next door or the cross walk on the other side. Here goes . . .'

'Hey,' he said, an hour or so later. 'I thought the boat and I were the ones to be photographed! But all you've taken so far are off-shore photographs of the Broadwater!'

'That's because I've never seen it from the water before,' she said enthusiastically. 'I love the Broadwater, I was only thinking about it last night . . .'

'What were you thinking about it?' he said idly.

She lowered her camera. 'I was wondering . . . if you were planning to go over the bar.'

'We could. Doesn't that appeal to you?'

'It scares me a little,' she said honestly. 'Even without Spider's tales of gloom, it does seem . . . a bit dangerous.'

They had anchored off the Southport Pool after doing a tour right round and back. And they'd put up the canvas awning on the back deck and were having a cup of coffee.

He smiled slightly. 'With the power we've got here plus the fact that I've crossed that bar more times than I'd care to remember—the years march on—' he said wryly, 'you'd have nothing to worry about. Who's Spider?'

'An . . . old man I know.'

'Dozens of boats go over the bar every day. Tell him that.'

'He . . . when you're old, you . . . how can I explain it? You talk and that's about all that's left to you. He thinks he's very knowledgeable. Besides, accidents do happen, don't they?'

'Oh yes. All right, we won't go over the bar. I wasn't planning to, anyway. I thought we'd cruise up to Tippler's, find a spot and anchor and we could have dinner there tonight. It's only half an hour or so but we could stop and fish on the way. Do you like to fish, Leonie?'

'Well, I'm not very good at it.'

'I'll show you.'

'That was beginner's luck,' he said with a grin later in the afternoon. 'Definitely! In fact I'd go further and declare that that fish caught itself.'

'How can you say that! I went through all the motions, I . . . what kind of fish is it?'

'The biggest bloody flathead that's been caught in these parts for years, that's all,' he said wryly.

'Are they good to eat? It's not a very pretty fish.'

'They're very good to eat. Prettiness in a fish is relative.'

'How do you cook them?'

'Filleted and fried.'

'Well, if you showed me how to fillet it, and I fried it, wouldn't that save going to Tippler's for tea?'

'You're a good cook,' he said hours later. They

were anchored off Tippler's—a name that conjured up visions of stealthy drinkers forced out to sea in Leonie's mind.

She'd cooked the fish he'd filleted, in a light batter, and in the process discovered a well-stocked pantry and plenty of salad ingredients in the fridge. Also a bottle of wine and a tin of pears and fresh cream. The galley was equipped with a stove top with three plates, and a microwave oven.

She spooned up the last mouthful of pear and said a few moments later, 'It's a beautiful night.' They were eating at a folding table set up on the back deck beneath a nearly full moon and they even had a bug-zapper operating to deal with the mosquitoes and sandflies that might be wafting across from the mangroves on the light breeze. 'This is doing things in great style,' she added with a grin as a sizzling ping came from the zapper which was a special light designed to attract insects and roast them . . . 'Where does the power come from? A generator?'

'Mmm.' He lifted his glass and sipped his wine with his eyes on her. She felt her heart contract slightly because she knew from something in that look that the easy familiarity with which he'd treated her all day was about to end. Or become another kind of familiarity. And she wished suddenly that she didn't feel rather weary because she needed all her wits about her, she knew, to play this in just the right key. If she didn't, all her plans could amount to nought . . .

She took a deep breath and waited.

But he took his time. He refilled her glass then his own and said idly, 'Tell me somethng about yourself, Leonie.'

'What would you like to know?'

He shrugged. 'Apart from having the most beautiful eyes I've ever seen, and a lovely, graceful body which you claim you don't use indiscriminately,' the moonlight picked up a glint of mockery in his own eyes, 'I know nothing about you.'

'That's not quite true,' she replied and glanced at him with a hint of challenge. 'You know I don't like the idea of desecrating beautiful spots in the name of so-called free enterprise, like sand-mining in Moreton or Fraser . . .'

'So-called?' he interrupted.

'Well, I don't despise free enterprise as such. But how free is it when someone has to pay the price for it eventually? And I think in the case of mining, any kind of mining, the environment is much at stake. It seems senseless to me to take everything you can from the earth, or the sand, and leave behind an ecology so mutilated that it's good for nothing ever again. That's the larger issue, of course. The particular one at stake on Moreton Island is a question of aesthetics too. It's such a beautiful place and so many people appreciate it and love it because it's untouched, and want it to stay that way. Although,' she hesitated and grimaced faintly, 'sometimes they show that love in a funny way when they leave behind their litter and tear it up with four-wheel drives . . . But, I suppose it all boils down to the question of who really owns Moreton Island and places like it.'

'Not a government but the people?'

'I think so,' she said quietly. 'That article was my small way of saying it, too. Perhaps that says more about me than I could tell you . . .'

'Well, yes it does. But then I'd already gleaned that you were not a . . . passive passenger content to let life slide past you. And what I wanted to know was more in the line of particulars. How old you are for one thing, your background . . .'

'I'm twenty-four. I grew up in Townsville. My father was a doctor but both my parents are dead now. I have a . . . married sister living in Sydney. What else would you like to know?' she said flatly.

'Nothing that you're not willing to tell me, Leonie,' he replied drily after a moment.

She lifted her shoulders. 'I just don't see that it's of any importance. Now is what matters, I think.'

He drained his glass and set it down and stared at it. Then he lifted his eyes and said softly but a little grimly, 'And how are you going to handle "now", Leonie? I must confess I'm agog because I get the distinct impression that for us to fall on each other and leap into bed is not part of your plan. At least not tonight.'

'Is that how you like it?' she murmured with a glimmer of irony in her grey eyes. 'I've always thought these things were better taken slowly . . . The way you lead up to—it, is often, always, as important as the final act, don't you think?'

The moon which had slid behind a bank of streaky cloud to turn it silver, sailed out again, bright and white now, and she saw a glint of anger in Guy Richardson's eyes as he said, 'You have a very cutting tongue, my dear. I'm surprised you haven't . . . suffered some unpleasant consequences on account of it. But, to get back to my point, while you might feel you can dictate the . . . aesthetics of it—something you are hot on apparently, observing the aesthetics—we did make a bargain, a rather specific one.'

'I haven't forgotten.'

'Then you won't mind,' he stood up, 'if I at least set the ball rolling tonight?' he drawled.

She tensed inwardly but forced herself to relax and didn't resist when he drew her to her feet . . .

They stood facing each other about a foot apart, for what seemed like an age to Leonie. Then he let go of her hand and took her loosely into his arms. 'You're quite tall for a girl,' he murmured, 'but slight in all the right places.' He let his hands linger about her waist. 'Do you feel . . . all right in my arms?' he asked with a faintly derisive smile and drew her infinitesimally closer while his hands moved upwards lingeringly and intimately because all she had on over her bikini top was the dusky pink blouse.

She stared up at him. The top of her head came about level with his eyes. Then she tried to look downwards instinctively but he was too quick for her.

He withdrew one hand and captured her chin and forced her to look up again. 'We made a bargain about that, too, if you recall,' he said, his lips barely moving. 'You can't really expect me to go through with this completely blindfolded, Leonie, you know,' he went on. 'And your eyes are about my only clue. The only chance I have of— for instance—telling if you're hating this . . .'

She blinked and said after the barest hesitation, 'Why should I be hating it?'

'You tell me. You're not exactly reciprocating— all I had in mind was kissing you.'

'I . . . th-then why don't you?' she said with the slightest tremor in her voice.

'Oh *hell*,' he answered with a sudden savagery and let her go. 'Forgive me,' he added, mockingly, 'but I'd rather not feel as if I was about to rape you.'

Leonie closed her eyes briefly. Then she said, 'I'm sorry. It's not that . . .'

He raised his eyebrows sceptically.

But she went on, although a little uncertainly. 'I . . . you . . . the plain truth is I'm . . . really tired.' And as she spoke a very real wave of exhaustion washed over her so that her shoulders slumped and she reached out a hand to grasp the back of her chair as a delayed reaction to the motion of the boat overcame her also.

His eyes narrowed. 'You are, too,' he said abruptly and put his hands on her shoulders as if he was afraid she would fall. 'Why?' he asked scanning her suddenly pale face.

'I guess I'm not used to boats for one thing,' she said with an effort. 'And I didn't get much sleep last night . . .' She broke off and bit her lip and her eyes flew to his before she could stop herself.

'So you did have some qualms, after all,' he murmured.

It seemed pointless to deny it but she wished desperately she hadn't given herself away . . . wished desperately at the same time that she could extricate herself from this situation which she was not handling very well. Guy Richardson was not going to be quite the piece of cake she'd visualised, at the best of times, she thought dazedly. He was far too acute for one thing . . .

Then the silence of the night around them was cut by the reverberating roar of an outboard motor being started up near by and she gasped and jumped and would have fallen if he hadn't lifted her up in a swift movement and held her close before letting her slide to her feet, although he still held her.

'It was only a boat,' he said wryly. 'Your heart's going like a train . . .'

'I just . . . got a fright,' she said huskily into his shoulder. 'It was so loud and so . . . unexpected.'

'And there he goes,' he said lifting his head as a runabout with a blinding spotlight cut a swathe through the water nearby and the *Marie-Claire* began to rock as its wake spread across the silver surface of the water. 'A fisherman by the look of the light. Come . . . I think you *might* have had enough for one day, Miss Powell,' he said and lifted her into his arms.

She didn't resist. Just lay quiet as he carried her down to Claire's cabin and laid her on the bed.

Then he said briefly, 'Hang on. I'll be back.'

Which he was in about two minutes with a tot of brandy. 'It's good for nerves, settling stomachs—you name it. Drink it down.'

She did with his arm about her, supporting her, then he laid her back and straightened up. 'Try and relax,' he said. 'I have no designs on you tonight but if you're worried you could always lock the door. And, well, tomorrow's another day, isn't it? If you're feeling better we could . . . resume hostilities then. *If* that's what this is all about,' he said with a certain dryness and went out, closing the door behind him.

Leonie didn't stir for a long time. Just stared at the door which was opposite the bed. Then she fell asleep without even changing.

CHAPTER THREE

IT was a shout that awakened her the next morning. Then a chorus of voices and the unmistakable movement of people climbing aboard the boat.

She frowned and glanced at her watch and blinked because it was nearly ten o'clock. She lay still for a while but all she could hear was what sounded like a lot of voices talking at once and enthusiastically. Visitors obviously, she mused. But planned visitors? I wonder . . .

Bu the dilemma she found herself in then—whether to stay put or not—was solved by the sound of Guy Richardson calling down the stairway apparently.

'Leonie! Time to get up, sleepy-head. Unless you want to be invaded down there. Some friends have arrived and they want to see over the boat.'

She sat up abruptly. ". . . Just give me a few minutes.'

She took about twenty to have a shower, dress and tidy the cabin. Then she stopped in front of the mirror and looked at herself. She wore fresh white shorts and a strapless, figure-hugging, cotton stretch-knit top in a clear, buttercup yellow and had tied her hair back with a yellow scarf. Both the shorts and the top were almost regulation dress for all females but the very old in a Queensland summer.

But Leonie experienced a period of disquiet which she identified as an urge to cover herself more. Now I wonder why? she reflected. That would look strange, if anything, on a day like this—sunlight was pouring through the portholes above.

And to give herself a bit more time . . . to gird my limbs, metaphorically? she asked herself with a sudden flash of humour in her eyes as she sat down at the dressing-table and examined her now uniformly tanned hands.

What you mean is, time to get your act together, Leonie, she told herself. If I remember it fell apart a little last night. Not that it did much harm really but it obviously made him curious. What do they say about curiosity?

'It killed the cat . . .'

She stared at herself in the mirror as her lowly spoken words seemed to echo round the cabin eerily. Her skin looked smooth and golden and perhaps because she'd taken a cold shower, her face had none of the puffiness of someone who had slept for twelve hours straight.

It was not so much a pretty face that stared back at her, as an elegant one—as someone had once told her. And added, with a rare flash of insight for him, that it was the kind of face that would stand the test of time well because of her good bones and her eyes . . .

'Yes, well,' she said with some decision and stood up, 'we'll see if I can't baffle you with my eyes yet, Mr Richardson. And so battle then, Leonie!'

But she had to grin faintly to herself because it sounded so dramatic said aloud like that . . .

'Oh now!' a male voice said admiringly into the sudden lull that greeted Leonie as she stood at the top of the stairs hesitantly. 'Oh, I say! Now we *really* know why Guy took off on this little cruise with not a word to anyone. How do you do, my dear?'

The speaker was a middle-aged little man with a bald head and bright snapping eyes and he moved forward to offer her his hand. 'I'm Bob Turner, by the way,' he went on. 'You know, this is an amazing coincidence. Peggy and I, and Brad and Laurel,' he gestured, 'were just cruising up to Russel Island to watch the speed boat races. Bored to tears we were really, when Brad happened to open his eyes to take a squint at the world—a thing he does rarely unless there are horses around—and he sat bolt upright, knocked over his beer, mind, and he said, "By God! That's Guy's new boat or I'm a Dutchman!" Didn't you, Brad?'

The second man in the group—Leonie had managed to work out that there were only four extra people aboard—tipped his large hat to her which he hadn't seen fit to remove even inside and looked sheepish.

In fact, she thought, he had a generally sheepish air about him, but not so much of nature as aura. He looked like everyone's favourite conception of a sheep shearer, even to his enormous, calloused hands. He also had very blue eyes.

And her first impressions of him seemed to be confirmed by his slow way of speaking. 'Well, ma'am,' he said, 'I did but I wish I hadn't. Can quite understand why Guy wanted some privacy ... um ... oh damn. I mean,' he scratched his face, 'I mean, I *said* to 'em, I said, look, you can bet your bottom dollar there's some reason for Guy to be sitting in the middle of Tippler's

Passage in his new boat and if he didn't tell us he was a-goin' cruising, that's his business . . .'

'I am not sitting in the *middle* of Tippler's Passage, Brad,' Guy said with a grin. 'And given another half an hour I'd have given you mob the slip, believe me. But anyway, this is Leonie. Leonie, you've met Bob—give her hand back, mate—and this is Bob's wife, Peggy.'

He motioned to a grey-haired woman with calm, humorous eyes who had been staring at Leonie with a slight frown of puzzlement. But she smiled then, warmly.

'And this is Laurel,' Guy went on, 'and the man who did all the damage, Brad Hawthorn. Laurel and Brad go together by the way. They're,' his eyes glinted suddenly, 'soul mates.'

Laurel Jones interrupted her curious, all-encompassing study of Leonie to glance at Guy reproachfully and say in a deep, throaty voice, 'Darling Guy, don't be mean. I like the look of your . . . soul mate, by the way. She has class.'

There was a suddenly uncomfortable silence as everyone looked at Leonie to see how she would take this.

And in fact her eyes widened as they rested on the other woman and registered the fact that Laurel Jones was gorgeous in a way that her obviously dyed red hair and heavily made-up face didn't dim. She had the sultry kind of looks—heavily lidded green eyes and a fully curved, luscious mouth, that went well with all the artifice.

All the same, Leonie opened her mouth to say . . . you've got it wrong, we're just friends . . . But something prompted her to lift her grey eyes to Guy Richardson's face to intercept his look of wry but subtly challenging amusement.

She took an inward breath and turned back to Laurel and heard herself saying amazingly evenly, 'Thank you. You're very kind . . .'

But she missed Guy's reaction because Peggy Turner shook her head once and moved forward to say ruefully, 'You mustn't mind Laurel, my dear. She just . . . speaks her mind. And you are very lovely,' she added sincerely and went on, 'Now tell me honestly, do you mind us invading you like this? Because if you do we'll go away. But if you don't we could make a day of it! We have all been dying to get a ride on Guy's new boat but even more, it would give us a chance to get to know each other. What do you think?'

For the life of her, Leonie couldn't resist glancing at Guy Richardson again but with a look of cool, ironic amusement in her own eyes as she said, 'That sounds like fun. If Guy doesn't mind, I think I'd like that . . .'

'Leonie,' Laurel said musingly in her deep husky voice. 'I like that name. It suits you, too. Have you known Guy long?'

Leonie considered before replying. They were up on the foredeck, leaning back against the galley windows as the *Marie-Claire* slipped through the water gently.

It was about mid-afternoon and they'd watched the speed boats hurtle past, Guy's new boat had been put through her paces at full speed, too, with her bow rearing high and the spray from the racing water beneath flying back exhilaratingly. They'd lunched with contributions from the picnic hamper off the Turners' boat, a sleek fast launch that had been tied on a long line so that it trailed behind the *Marie-Claire*. And now Peggy was lying down, having claimed with a twinkle in her eye that the one thing she had earned at her time of life, was the right to take a kip after lunch. And Laurel and Leonie had come up on to the foredeck to sunbathe—the men were up on the fly deck, talking idly of boats and horsepower and fishing.

'Not long,' Leonie said.

'Do you mind me asking? You took so long to answer.'

'I ... no,' Leonie said and discovered that she didn't from one point of view. For over the last hours, she'd found herself observing Laurel Jones and coming to the conclusion that she was not bitchy or catty as first impressions might have led one to believe, but one of those ultra-genuine people who did simply speak their minds at all times. And her lips trembled into a smile as she considered the discomfort this obviously caused her friends from time to time.

'No,' she said again, 'I don't really.'

'Then you're going through the horrors with Guy. I mean,' Laurel said, 'I just get the impression you two are not quite on the same wavelength. Men,' she added, 'can do that to you *par excellence*.'

'That's ... not quite true. I haven't known Guy long enough for that.'

Laurel Jones slid eyes round to Leonie and tilted her head a fraction so that she could see from beneath the peak of her sun-hat. 'Want to tell me about it?' she enquired.

Leonie hesitated. 'There's not much to tell ...'

'Guy,' Laurel said meditatively then, 'would not be the easiest man to ... love. I've seen a few come and go over the six or so years I've known him. Of course I didn't know his wife, Marie. She died of some incurable disease unfortunately when Claire was only little. One wonders if he's ever got over it. Brad knew her. She was French and just ... bewitching apparently. They appeared to be the ideal couple. I must say I cherished a little crush on Guy myself once. But then I was only a naïve little hairdresser in those days and I had a crush on the whole rarefied atmosphere of the super-rich which I'd stumbled into.'

'Hawthorn ... and Turner,' Leonie said slowly.

'Mmm ... Brad made his money out of meat and Bob out of real estate. That's one nice thing about the Gold Coast though, don't you think, Leonie? I mean it's the money you've made that counts, not the fact that you were a butcher once ...'

Leonie couldn't help laughing.

'Of course,' Laurel went on, 'Brad has diversified, particularly into racehorses and if you want to hobnob with ... let's say *pedigreed* society, that's one sure way to do it, especially if you're as successful as Brad is. But I think if there's one thing I love most about Brad, it's that at heart, he's still a simple man. In every respect but one.'

'What's that?'

'He's capable of loving two women at the same time. Me and his wife.'

'I'm sorry,' Leonie said after a moment.

'Yes, it is a bit sad,' Laurel agreed. 'Because it means that I've joined that faceless league of women known as mistresses—not something I really wanted to do to myself. Oh, it hasn't been as bad for me as some. I've gone ahead and built a career for myself, with Brad's help. I *own* my own beauty salon now and I've paid him back every

cent he lent me to do it. I'm also—something of an
identity in my own right, something of a trend-
setter,' she said with a curiously wry little smile.
'But I still lack the privileges of a wife. And I'm
still the target of . . . barbed remarks from people
some of whom I even like and respect—like Guy
this morning. But then I've always known he's
something of a puritan at heart.'

Leonie stirred. 'Is he?'

'Oh, I think so . . .'

'You did say just now that you'd seen a few
women come and go . . . Is that puritanical?'

'Ah, but there's a subtle difference with Guy.
His affairs are always on the level. He never, that
I've known, gets involved with married women.'

Leonie narrowed her grey eyes and looked
piercingly at the other woman for a moment. Until
Laurel raised her eyebrows. 'What's wrong? Don't
tell me you're . . .'

'No,' Leonie said hastily and changed tack. In
truth, she thought as she spoke, she had been a
little moved by the other woman's honesty. 'But,
from Brad's point of view, perhaps he has a
family—perhaps that's why he . . .'

'Won't divorce her and marry me? You know,
the funny thing is, if he'd . . . been less faithful to
us, if he had a lot of other women, I'd have
agreed. But much as it . . . hurts me, and possibly
her, I've come to believe he loves us both. Perhaps
there's something in me that's missing in her and
vice versa.'

'I'm sorry,' Leonie said sincerely.

Laurel smiled and touched her hand. 'Thank
you. You're sweet. And forgive me for trying to
pry into . . . whatever it is you have going with
Guy. I'm afraid it's becoming a habit with me.

One of the morbid consequences of being a mistress, no doubt. It seems to make you quite avid to know how other people's love affairs prosper. Or perhaps it's one of the consequences of getting old!'

'Old!' Leonie echoed.

'Uh-huh. I'll be thirty soon. Think of that . . .'

'Think of what?' Bob Turner called with his head popped over the edge of the fly deck. 'What are you two girls discussing so seriously down there?'

'Nothing to do with you, Bob,' Laurel called back cheerfully. 'Listen, why don't you ask Guy when he's going to stop showing off his boat and pull her up so that we can have a swim? Leonie and I are cooking and there's a lovely little beach just passing by on his port bow. Tell him he could anchor in the roads like the Queen Mary and we could go over in your boat.'

'I heard that, Laurel,' Guy said. 'But you're wrong about one thing, it's my starboard bow.'

'Port, starboard it all means nothing to me, pet,' Laurel said cheerfully and grinned at Leonie, her eyes full of mischief. 'Men are like little boys about their boats, had you noticed?'

'I heard that, too,' Guy said from above. 'Pity about that. It was a nice little beach, wasn't it?'

'Oh, Guy!' Laurel wailed. 'I was only teasing you. I take it all back! You ask him, Leonie! Wouldn't you like a swim?'

'I'd love one . . .'

'Well, now, that's a different matter . . .' And almost immediately the *Marie-Claire* could be felt to be slowing down.

*   *   *

'You're a good swimmer.'

'Thank you,' Leonie said. She was floating on her back in fairly shallow water, about shoulder height for Guy Richardson who'd approached with a powerful crawl and stood up beside her.

She felt for the bottom herself but it was just too deep for her to stand. 'I . . .'

'Here.' He took her in his arms and smiled slightly as she instinctively tried to free herself, then stopped uncertainly. 'I made one resolution for today, Leonie,' he said softly but with his eyes glinting wickedly. 'Only one. That I would kiss you come hell or high water. And I think this is the time for it.' He moved a bit so that she could stand but didn't let go of her.

She put up a hand to brush the wet strands of hair from her eyes and trod on a stone, and found herself clutching his wet shoulder with that hand.

'Steady,' he said. 'What was that?'

'A stone. I don't . . . think I want to be kissed in public . . .' she tried to say evenly but her mind registered the fact that she'd sounded curiously breathless.

'Oh, they won't mind,' he said with an inclination of his head towards the beach. 'In fact, they're probably expecting it.'

'Then let's be different. Let's disappoint them.

'But the thing is, my lovely mermaid,' Guy Richardson drawled, 'if *you* don't start to deliver soon, *I* might start to believe just that. That you're only a will o' the wisp, a siren who lures men into a trap, a mermaid . . .'

Leonie was silent, cornered, she thought.

'All right,' she said quietly at last and lifted her mouth.

His lips were cool and firm and gentle. But as

they touched hers, she couldn't stop herself from trembling slightly down the length of her body in a way that could have been anticipation, or fear. And for an instant, he hesitated, and then his mouth left hers and instead, he kissed the line of her jaw lightly and slid his tongue into the hollow below her ear. Then those wandering lips traced a path down the side of her neck, kissing, tasting, exploring the damp, cool skin at the base of her throat, along the line of her shoulder . . .

Leonie closed her eyes and unconsciously spread the fingers of her hand that was still resting on his shoulder and found herself *feeling* with it, feeling his own cool, damp skin, the muscles beneath that moved as he moved his head and let his tongue glide back to her throat.

She tilted her head back instinctively, then stopped and tensed as she realised what she'd done. He stopped, too, but didn't lift his head, only held her in both arms with their bodies only just touching in a curved embrace that had a curious delicacy about it.

Perhaps it's the water, she found herself thinking dazedly. Something has to be . . . making it feel like nothing else I've ever known, like a body poem . . .

She moved her hand tentatively on his shoulder, and found herself relaxing then unwittingly, softening somehow, and tilting her head back again. And he began to kiss her again, slowly and with an open mouth down towards the hollow between her breasts.

Oh God, she thought dimly, and made a small inarticulate sound in her throat of something like despair and he lifted his head at last but only to claim her lips this time . . .

And then she realised she was powerless to resist him but what was worse perhaps, was the way she felt herself responding.

Even when the wash of a large boat floated them off their feet towards the shore and they came to rest in the shallows, half lying in the water with her uppermost but still kissing him with her hand now on his cheek . . .

It took the sharp braying of a hooter and a chorus of catcalls and whistles to make her lift her head abruptly to see a cruise boat receding with all the passengers waving energetically at . . . She looked around. At her . . . them, because there was no-one else in the water . . .

'Oh!' she gasped and tried to wrench herself out of Guy Richardson's arms and then when she realised he was laughing, she tried to slap his face as a swift uprush of possibly illogical anger claimed her.

'Leonie . . .'

'Don't Leonie me,' she said fiercely. 'You might like to be a laughing-stock . . . let me go!' She looked pointedly and coldly at her wrist which he'd captured in one long, strong hand.

'In a moment,' he said, still grinning and pushed off from the beach with his legs and with his other arm about her waist.

'What are you *doing*?'

'I wasn't laughing at *you*.'

'Everyone else w-was,' she retorted somewhat indistinctly as she swallowed some water and then began to thrash around in a sort of panic.

'Leonie . . .' He stopped paddling idly and towing her along, and he stood up, drawing her to her feet in a spot where the water was about waist high. 'Don't . . .' He frowned down at her.

'I . . .' She bit her lip and felt her face flush and her body go weak in a strange way, as if from reaction. 'I'm sorry,' she said numbly. 'I suppose it must have looked funny.'

'It didn't feel funny,' he said quietly and touched her mouth with two fingers. 'It felt very good.'

'All the same you . . .' She shrugged.

'All the same I laughed,' he agreed. 'I know, but because that's the first time in my life I've been caught kissing someone so . . . very intently that it took a boat hooter to bring me back to earth.'

'You were the one who didn't mind doing it in public.'

'Not quite that publicly,' he said wryly then sobered. 'But you were the one who thought she didn't like to do it all all, Leonie. Am I wrong . . .?'

'I . . . yes, you're wrong,' she whispered.

'Look at me, Leonie.'

'No . . .' She caught her breath. 'All right.' She lifted her grey eyes to his defiantly. 'What does that tell you?'

'Nothing,' he answered drily. 'As you don't intend it to. But then perhaps enough is enough— for today. At least I've achieved what I set out to do. Don't,' he said again as she stiffened.

'I . . .'

'Yes you are—going all tense. Relax. I generally stick to my word. Let's see if we can enjoy the rest of this day. Come . . .' He put his arms around her waist from behind and after a moment of resistance, she leant back against him and he floated off, still holding her with her legs between his, his body cradling hers and the now still water just lapping them gently.

And Leonie found herself unexpectedly soothed
. . . It's like being caressed, she thought, but so . . .
peacefully . . .

'Hey!' A shout came from close by and a wave
of water washed over them so that they sank a
little and both came up spluttering.

'Hell,' Guy Richardson said with a grin, his
dark hair plastered wetly to his head but with his
blue eyes glinting with amusement. 'Is there no
peace for the wicked? Okay? I think the others are
coming to . . . well, coming.'

'Mmm. I'm . . . okay,' she answered and looked
over his shoulder. 'And you're right. We're about
to be bombarded. I think escape might be the best
means of defence . . .'

'Swim for your life, then . . .'

She did.

'Brought this over too!' Bob said flourishing
Leonie's guitar. 'Guy reckons you're the musician,
Leonie. How about a tune now we've eaten?'

Leonie grimaced, then reached for the in-
strument and started to unzip the case.

They'd decided to have a barbecue on the beach
after their swim. Guy had produced chops and
steak from the galley fridge and a barbecue grid
without which, he said, he never travelled. And
while the men had got a fire going on the beach,
Leonie and Peggy and Laurel had made some
salads on the *Marie-Claire*, then Bob had ferried
them back to the beach and produced a bottle of
wine from his cool box, which they drank out of
paper cups while they ate their meat with their
fingers.

'Yum!' Laurel had declared. 'There's nothing
like meat cooked over a wood fire for flavour!'

The sun had gone down behind them and now the firelight was casting flickering shadows on the sand and the trees that edged the beach. They'd rinsed the dishes, and themselves, in the salt water and packed most of the gear back into Bob's boat and Peggy was pouring coffee from a flask into more paper cups.

'Add a tot of this,' Brad said lazily and produced a small bottle of rum.

Peggy grinned but did as she was bid.

Leonie sipped hers and then settled herself more comfortably against the smooth rock that was her backrest and began to strum idly. Presently a tune formed and with a slight smile, she began to sing . . . 'What shall we do with a drunken sailor? What shall we do with a drunken sailor? What shall we do with a drunken sailor early in the morning . . .'

It was Peggy who took over in a lovely clear soprano and she obviously knew all the words so the rest of them were able to devote themselves to the chorus, and did so enthusiastically and gratifyingly.

'Oh that was lovely!' Peggy said, her kindly face glowing in the firelight. 'Takes me back to my girlhood. What else do you know, Leonie?'

Leonie glanced around at the circle of faces to see everyone looking at her expectantly so she began to strum again.

They sang a mixture of sad songs, love songs, old favourites, *Waltzing Matilda* with Brad unexpectedly leaping up to go through the motions and sending them all into fits of laughter. Then finally they fell silent and let her play just idly for a time, each of them apparently wrapped up in their own thoughts . . .

Peggy and Bob were holding hands, Brad was

lying back with Laurel in his arms resting her cheek on his shoulder and staring into the firelight and Guy Richardson, well he was doing the same, Leonie noticed from beneath her lashes, staring into the firelight.

He was sitting beside her with his arms clasped around his knees and he was so still, she wondered what he was thinking about. Something . . . far away, she thought. Claire perhaps? Or . . . his dead wife, Marie?

She stopped playing with one last, soft chord. And for a moment no-one moved. Then Peggy sighed and Laurel turned her lips to Brad's shoulder and Guy put out his hand on the sand beside her.

Leonie hesitated then slipped her own hand into it and felt his fingers close gently about hers.

It was Bob who brought them all back from their private dream worlds.

'Honey,' he said sincerely to Leonie, 'that was beaut. Thank you.'

'A pleasure,' she murmured.

'I suppose you're going to tell us we ought to get going now,' Peggy said to her husband with a grimace.

Bob stretched. 'Well it is Monday tomorrow. Back to the salt mines for some of us! Uh . . . Guy excepted.'

Guy looked up from the fire for the first time and grinned. 'Some salt mine you operate from, old mate,' he said.

'Yes,' Laurel agreed. 'Way up there above Surfer's with all that air-conditioning and genuine leather and glass and chrome . . .'

And they were all wrangling then but amicably, like the good friends they obviously were and for a moment Leonie felt her heart contract because she was sure one of them was going to ask her what kind of a salt mine hers was but no-one did, although Guy looked at her curiously and she realised he must have felt that moment of tension through her hand that he still held.

But the awkward moment passed as they all clambered aboard Bob's boat for the short trip back to the *Marie-Claire*. Then there was a general sorting out of gear and a discussion about whether there would be enough water where the *Marie-Claire* was anchored when the tide went out or if she should be moved for the night—it was decided she need not be—and finally, farewells, made by each and everyone of Guy Richardson's friends with a degree of warmth that took Leonie a little by surprise.

'I'm just *so* happy to have met you, my dear,' Peggy said and kissed her and then Bob insisted on being accorded the same privilege. 'Hope we see a lot more of you. In fact if we don't, I shall want to know why!' he declared.

'Hear, hear!' Laurel agreed and kissed Leonie, too. 'Come and see me sometime, Leonie,' she added. 'Or better still, give me a ring and we could have lunch together one day. But don't go through all the Joneses in the book. Just look up the Laurelei Beauty Salon. Now I mean that!'

'Thanks, I'd like to . . .'

'Well, Leonie,' Brad said smothering one of her hands in his vast one, 'can't say I'm sorry for spying Guy's new boat after all. It's been great to meet you, my word it has. I'd even say that you cast the *Marie-Claire* into the shade . . .'

'Wow! That's praise!' Laurel observed with a grin. 'Not the highest mind, but pretty close to it.'

'What could be higher than that?' Guy queried.

'Nothing, coming from you, probably. But from Brad the highest accolade is when he tells you you remind him of a little filly he once had that won the Oaks or . . .'

'I like your friends,' Leonie said.

The sound of Bob's boat had died away into the distance and all that could be heard was the water lapping the side of the boat and the occasional plop of a fish jumping. The moon was not as bright as it had been the night before but still shedding enough light to create angular shadows on the back deck.

Leonie was standing in one such shadow, Guy out in the moonlight, leaning against a white-painted stanchion.

'Thanks . . . They like you.'

She hesitated, watching his tall figure still clad only in shorts as it had been all day, outlined in silver but somehow dark and remote looking within the outline. And thought that he still hadn't quite come back from those far away thoughts he'd been thinking earlier on the beach . . . Either that or he was not best pleased with the prospect of the night that lay ahead.

She took a breath and said with a catch in her voice, 'Would you like something? A drink, a . . . nightcap?'

He didn't speak for a moment, then he turned towards her and said, 'No. I guess it's bed-time. Good-night, Leonie.'

Leonie never knew what prompted her to do what she did. It just seemed to be a gesture she found herself making quite naturally . . .

She walked soft-footed across to him and stood

for a moment in front of him with the moonlight striking through the cloudy chiffon of her sarong and revealing her figure beneath in one of her new bikinis, the swell of her breasts, the curve of her hips, but giving it a shadowy ephemeral quality.

And she said very quietly, 'Good night, Guy. Thank you for a lovely day . . .'

She stood up on her toes and took his head between her hands and kissed him on the lips.

He did nothing for an instant. Then when her mouth left his, he linked his hands loosely about her waist and said very quietly himself, 'Thank *you* for that. A little . . . trust, goes a long way. Sleep well, my dear.' And he released her.

She stared up into his eyes, but they were dark and unreadable. So she dipped her head in some sort of grateful acknowledgement, and turned and vanished into the cabin like a shadow . . .

She took a shower before going to bed.

And then found herself sitting in front of the dressing-table in her lilac terry robe and brushing her hair with a curious feeling of *déjà vu*.

This is where I started out this morning, she thought. Slightly confused then, which is nothing to what I am now—and prepared for battle I was this morning, yet, or so it seems, with a wrong conception of the real enemy . . .

'Or,' she said beneath her breath, 'unaware that there were two enemies. Guy Richardson . . . and myself.'

She sighed and reached for the expensive body lotion she'd bought especially for this trip, and turning round, began to smooth it on to her legs.

I was quite sure I could . . . fake anything that was required of me, she mused. Up to a point, naturally. Yet all I could manage was to be stiff and tense . . .

'And lead him to wonder what the hell was going on.' The murmured words escaped her involuntarily. '*Then*,' she whispered with her hands stilled about one ankle and a strangely hot and cold sensation flooding her, 'to get *so* carried away, lose every ounce of poise like a silly schoolgirl . . . how did it happen?'

She sat like that for a few minutes, reliving the unexpected effects Guy Richardson's kiss and embrace had had on her in the water.

Then she slipped her robe off and smoothed the lotion over the rest of her body deftly and swiftly and reached for her nightgown and slipped into Claire's pretty little bed. But even switching the lamp off didn't stop her thoughts.

He can't really be a puritan at heart, she reflected staring upwards to the open porthole that was channelling a diffused stream of moonlight into the cabin. I *know* he's not despite what Laurel said . . . I know better. What I didn't take into account was the fact that he's . . . likeable. And that might have been a tactical error of rather serious proportions . . .

CHAPTER FOUR

IT was a grey, muggy day that greeted them the next morning with swollen, lowering clouds hanging overhead and a humidity reading that would come close to a hundred per cent.

'Phew!' Leonie said after she'd cooked breakfast of bacon and eggs. 'I'm in a lather of sweat!'

'Me, too. It must rain today. Not the the best day for taking photos, perhaps,' Guy Richardson said idly.

Leonie glanced at him. He was sitting at the walnut table drinking a cup of tea and it had been a curiously unemotional meeting this morning. Leonie had come up from her cabin feeling strangely shy and predictably nervous. To find she'd woken first although only by about ten minutes. No sooner than she'd arrived in the upper cabin, she'd heard the shower going downstairs and he'd appeared not much later with his hair damp and the look about him of someone rather out of tune with the world.

So she'd cooked breakfast quickly and competently and silently. And she heard herself say then, as she sipped her tea, too, and stared out at the dull view, 'If ... would you rather we called it off?'

'Called what off, Leonie?' he said after a while.

She turned back from her contemplation of the grey, silent waterway beyond the galley windows. 'The whole thing. The article, this ... you and I.'

'Isn't it going the way you planned?'

'It's . . . not that,' she said and lifted a hand in a gesture of rather impatient helplessness because of course it was that in a way. The past night had shown her that in the form of doubts and second thoughts and the growing feeling that she might not be able to go through with this. The problem was, how to express herself without giving herself away . . . In fact, would it be so terrible if I did that? she pondered. It could be if I lost my job. But then I was prepared for that, and prepared to count it well lost. But this way I've achieved . . . nothing . . .

'What is it then?' His words cut through her thoughts abruptly.

'I . . .' she hesitated, 'thought you looked—not too happy about things this morning,' she said with a shrug. Which was true, too. But then, again, she found herself subject to an impulse as she had been last night when she'd kissed him good night. 'As a matter of fact,' she said slowly then went on in a rush, 'I wondered if you'd had some unhappy memories resurrected for you, somehow.'

'What do you mean?' His voice was curt and his dark blue eyes frowning.

'I . . . I'm not quite sure. You—well after we sang on the beach last night you . . . just seemed to have been very *introspective* since, if that's the right word. Songs—music,' she added a little lamely, 'have the greatest power of association . . . for me, anyway. They bring back to mind people, places, all sorts of things. Your . . . wife, perhaps,' she said and immediately wished she hadn't. 'I'm sorry . . .'

'What do you know of my wife?' he said tautly.

'Nothing. Only . . .' She bit her lip and cursed herself inwardly. 'Only what Laurel told me yesterday. That she'd died when—not long after . . .'

'Bloody Laurel,' he said coldly and cuttingly. 'I sometimes think she *thinks* because she's nobody's wife, she can go around prying and poking . . .' He stopped. 'How the hell did Marie come up anyway?'

'Because Laurel assumed, as they all did yesterday, that you and I were . . . lovers,' Leonie said steadily. 'An impression you did nothing to dispel,' she added.

'Nor you, Leonie,' he retorted mockingly. 'Anyway, what they assumed is only an anticipation of the fact, isn't it? Or isn't it? I still cherish some doubts about that if you don't mind my saying so.' He looked at her with his mouth set in a hard line.

'I. . .' She stopped and bit her lip again.

'Oh for God's sake,' he said savagely, 'forget that. The complexities of it are beyond me this early in the morning, I'm afraid. But I still don't see how you and Laurel came to be discussing Marie.'

Leonie contained an inward shiver. He looked so angry and impatient. And she strove to make her voice cool and calm. 'The last thing I wanted to do was discuss your wife with anyone, believe me. But Laurel,' she shrugged, 'went further than just making that initial assumption. She . . . detected that you and I were not quite in accord and she asked me about it. I denied it and . . . tried to be vague and that's when she started to talk about Marie, and you. It just came about as a result of . . . circumstances,' she said levelly.

'I don't know why she doesn't set herself up as a one-woman lonely hearts club,' he retorted acidly. 'I suppose she told you her own sad story, too?'

'Yes. All the same I liked her,' Leonie said and frowned at her cup.

'Does that—you say that as if you really feel you shouldn't. I wonder why, Leonie?' His voice was suddenly mocking. 'Are you a puritan at heart?'

She lifted her eyes to his with a look of quizzical wryness in them, and thought, how ironic . . .

'And what's that supposed to mean,' he asked swiftly and intently. 'Something you find humorous?'

She started to look down and forced herself to stop. 'I suppose I do in a way. Not—obviously not because I'm a puritan,' she said gently, 'but because I can't help wondering if many men don't have double standards in that respect.'

'Go on,' he said dangerously.

'Well, you seem to have a down on Laurel but not on Brad. Now I, too, curiously,' her voice was suddenly very steady, 'feel that anyone who intrudes into a marriage is violating something they ought not to. But in Brad's case it seems to me Laurel is copping all the flak . . .' She stopped suddenly and bit her lip and a strange expression came to her eyes, as if she was examining something far away, something puzzling.

It was his restless movement that brought her back to say less certainly, 'But Laurel is genuinely in love with Brad, I think . . .'

'That may be,' Guy said tersely after a while. 'So is his wife.'

'Well, what it boils down to, I guess, is that you think Laurel should give Brad up, while I think . . .'

'It should be the other way around,' he said flatly.

'Not *necessarily*.' She frowned. 'I think, why blame one more than the other? In *that* particular case. Actually,' she added with an effort, 'that's quite a departure from my normal way of thinking . . .'

'Because you are a puritan after all?'

'Because,' she looked at him, 'I'm a bit more sensitive about it I guess, than some. My father left my mother for another woman, for one thing. And I knew someone else who . . . well, threw up her marriage for another man, then found she had nothing. But, and I suppose Laurel made me realise this yesterday, it's easy to theorise and moralise until it happens to you. In *some* cases . . .'

She stopped abruptly then turned towards the sink with a shrug and emptied her tea cup. But she lifted her head as the sound of an outboard motor disturbed the humid stillness of the morning, and saw a small aluminium runabout streak into view only to hit some unseen object in the water apparently, and rear up and dislodge its occupants into the water.

'Oh, my God!' she gasped. 'Look . . .'

He was on his feet beside her, but one comprehensive glance through the galley window was enough. 'How many?' he fired at her and shoved her out on to the back deck where the *Marie-Claire*'s own dinghy hung from two winches.

'Four, I think,' she said shakily, 'Kids, I think . . .'

'Grab those extra life-jackets and put one on . . .'

'But they might need them. I can swim . . .'

'Just *do* it, Leonie . . .'

He had the dinghy in the water in an unbelievably short time and the outboard clipped on and was priming it as she jumped in.

'Start, you bastard,' he snarled at it, 'don't play up on me today!'

The motor took the hint and roared into life. 'Keep your eyes peeled, Leonie,' he shouted. 'Here we go . . .'

The next—she didn't know how long—was like a nightmare Leonie found herself devoutly hoping she would never be called upon to relive. Two of the occupants of the now upturned and drifting runabout they located quite easily and hauled aboard shaken but apparently unharmed. Then they spied a third boy—they were all children barely into their teens—floating face down and Guy shoved the rudder into her hand and dived overboard with some instructions she didn't catch.

She closed her eyes because she had not the faintest idea how to drive the outboard. Then she turned to one of the boys, 'Tell me what to do! Do you know how to?'

'Yes,' he panted, 'it was my boat, my Dad's . . .'

'Then take us as close to them as you can but not . . .'

'I won't . . .'

'I think he's . . . just knocked out,' Guy panted as between them they lifted the inert body into the dinghy. 'Start artificial respiration though. Seen the other one?'

'No!'

'Then . . . tow me . . . back to . . . the runabout. Might be underneath it . . .'

They did and as he began to dive Leonie got to

work on the unconscious boy as best she could, desperately trying to recall all she knew about resuscitation. And to make matters worse it started to rain heavily. Then the boy she was working on sat up and coughed and at the same time Guy surfaced with another body in his arms.

'I think he's all right, too,' he shouted. 'There was a bubble of air but he started to panic and hit his head. Knocked out, too . . .'

'Oh, thank God,' she muttered. 'I'll start on him.' But this one must have only stunned himself because he came to without any assistance and started to vomit over the side of the boat. She turned back to Guy. 'Here . . . Guy!' she screamed, 'look out!' But it was too late.

A squall of rain, driven by a sharp gust of wind—the first breath of moving air so far in the morning—enveloped them and the up-turned boat swung round sharply and hit him on the back of the head. He coughed once and sank.

'Oh no. Oh God! Here,' she turned to the boy in control of the dinghy, 'just keep it out of the way in case of the propellor but watch *out* for us. I'm going in . . .'

And she scrambled over the side, unable to dive because of the life-jacket she wore but glad of it all the same because if only she could find him it would help to keep them both afloat . . .

'There! Over there!' A voice shouted and she turned to see one of the boys pointing. Guy had surfaced again but it was obvious he was in difficulties. She started to swim . . .

The next thing she really remembered was a voice saying, 'It's a bloody miracle . . . Bumps, scratches, bruises maybe but they're all all right otherwise.

Though Guy only just made it, I'd say. If it hadn't been for the sheila . . . Wonder which boat she was on? Guy's boat or the kid's?'

'Probably the *Maria-Claire*,' another voice said. 'I'd say she was a bit of a looker. Never saw Guy with one that wasn't . . . Coast Guard Two calling headquarters. Come in. Tom? Bill, mate. Look we've just effected a rescue, six people, two from Guy Richardson's new boat, I'd say, and four young hooligans who pinched one of their father's boats and went for a joy-ride . . . What's that? No. Not a mark on the *Marie-Claire* . . . too right, it would have been a bloody shame. No, the kids hit a drifting log from what we can gather, they're a bit shook up, and Guy went to the rescue off the *Marie-Claire* together with a sheila. In fact we've got them all on board her and that's where I'm calling from. Reckon I'll bring her into Runaway Bay. Can you have an ambulance standing by? What's that? No, nothing serious I reckon although Guy's still out like a light himself but he's breathing okay and the girl's just plain exhausted but best to get 'em all checked over. Nev'll bring our boat in and the runabout. What's that? Sure I know how to handle her! I was with him when she took her first sea trials . . . Okay, over and out, Tom!'

Leonie sat up dizzily having heard all this with not the slightest idea where she was. Now she saw that she had been lying on one of the padded cushions on the back deck of the *Marie-Claire* and the one-way conversation she'd been listening to had in fact been taking place on the fly deck. And everything that had been said suddenly fell into place and she bowed her head with a rush of relief.

Then she looked up again as two burly men

descended the ladder, both clad in khaki uniforms
with Coastguard epaulets.

'There,' the one who'd called himself Bill said,
coming over to her, 'perked up a bit have you?
You're one real brave lady, luv. And we'll have
you somewhere more comfortable in a tick.'

'Is he ... really all right?' she asked with
difficulty.

'He might have a sore head when he comes
round. But Guy's as tough as they come, don't
you worry.' He straightened. 'Right oh, Nev, see
you at the Marina.'

'Nev' climbed into the yellow Coastguard shark
cat and pushed off. 'As for you lot,' Bill said to
four scared looking teenage boys sitting in the
cabin around Guy Richardson's supine form,
'don't touch nothing and just sit tight. Don't
suppose your daddies are going to like this, no
more than I, but it could have been worse. You all
could have been drowned.' He turned away and
began to climb the ladder again muttering to
himself, 'I don't know. Kids! Not even a life-jacket
between 'em.'

'Oh!' Leonie recoiled. She'd come round a corner
in the hospital to bump into Bill from the
Coastguard of all people. It was late afternoon and
after insisting that Leonie rest in a cubicle in
Casualty for some hours, the doctor had now
authorised her release.

'Well, fancy seeing you again, ma'am,' Bill said
genially as he steadied her with a large hand. 'How
are you now?'

'I'm fine. Thank you very much—for everything,' she said huskily. 'I didn't get a chance
to . . .'

'That's okay, it's my job, luv. Actually I'm off duty now and I thought I'd just pop in to see how Guy was. He's a good mate of mine.'

'Well,' Leonie said, 'I've just spoken to the doctor and they're going to keep him in overnight. He's . . . in a private ward and they say it's only a precaution against concussion.' She didn't add that she herself hadn't seen Guy.

'That's good news then. Told you he was tough! Well, I guess he's sleeping it off so I won't disturb him. You . . . leaving now yourself?'

'Yes. Only I'm not quite sure how . . .' She looked down at herself still clad in the shorts and T-shirt she'd been in all day that had literally dried on her. 'I . . . thought. I could get a taxi and pay for it when I get there.'

'You going back to the *Marie-Claire*?'

'Well, all my things are there, and . . .'

'Of course! Now why didn't I think of that before. I've locked her up. You going to spend the night on her?'

'I . . . I'm not sure. But I do have to go back because I have not a cent on me and apart from my clothes, my wallet is there, too . . .'

'No problem!' Bill said, 'I'll drive you. I live at Hollywell anyway, right next door . . .'

And that was how Leonie got back to the *Marie-Claire*. In fact she had to fend off Bill's kind offers to drive her back into town in case she decided to, but it was a stroke of luck that she had bumped into him because she doubted if she'd have been able to get the key from the marina supervisor without authorisation, to get into the boat. Which would have meant spending the night at home then coming back the next morning—a thing that

didn't fit in with the plan that been growing in her
mind ever since she'd seen Guy Richardson being
wheeled away and had realised that nobody
seemed to take it amiss when she didn't press to be
with him, or see him . . .

I can go, she'd thought staring up at the sterile
white of the casualty department ceiling. I can . . .
disappear. He doesn't know where I live so he
couldn't trace me, anyway he probably won't want
to. And it would be a way to do it with no
explanations, no . . . nothing. And I think, her lips
had trembled, that's what you ought to do,
Leonie, before you get in over your head. This
wasn't such a good idea after all . . .

Only then, it had struck her that she might not
be able to go anywhere, let alone back to the
Marie-Claire.

Which means I owe you a second lot of thanks,
Bill, she thought as she stuck the key into the main
cabin door and turned to wave once more to Bill.

'Sure you'll be okay now? Hey,' he started to
lumber back, 'want me to hook you up to the
electricity on the pier? Here we go.' He unwound a
long extension lead and plugged it into the boat
and then to a dispenser on the pier. 'See how it's
done? Now if you change your mind and decide
not to spend the night here, just unplug her, lock
the door and hand the key in again.'

'You've been very kind, Bill. Really you have.
And don't tell me all this is part of your job,' she
said with a smile.

'Oh well, perhaps not,' he confessed. 'But I
reckon Guy would want any of his mates to do the
best they could for the girl who saved his life.'

'I'm sure I didn't . . .'

'I wouldn't be too sure of that! The only thing

that was between him and the bottom when we happened along, was you. Which I'll tell him next time I see him. Anyway, hooray for the time being, luv.'

And he did finally go this time.

Leonie let herself in and grimaced, because the cabin was in a bit of a mess. And she thought, I won't leave it like this. I've got plenty of time ... all night, although I won't take all night of course ...

In fact it only took her an about an hour to clean up the dirty stains on the carpet and cushions and wash the breakfast dishes. Then she found a hose on the pier and washed off the back deck. By which time the sun had set and she made herself a cup of coffee and thought of getting something to eat but found she didn't feel hungry.

I'll have a shower and pack, she thought, as she sipped her coffee. Then I'll lock up and ring for a taxi. Spider will be surprised to see me back so soon. What will I say? Oh I know, that we had an accident. Spider will love that ...

Half an hour later she was clean and dressed in her jeans and the blue silky blouse she hadn't had a chance to wear before, and had packed—some things rather ruefully, like her camera, and her bank book which she'd have been lost without, not to mention identifiable because it had her address on it.

And she stared at herself for one last time in the mirror, then looked away abruptly and picked up her bag and walked out of Claire Richardson's cabin.

But suddenly everything seemed to be an effort, so much so that she hoisted her bag up the four

steps that led to the galley instead of climbing up
with it, and leant her cheek against the smooth
walnut beside the steps . . .

And wondered if she'd done too much on top of
a traumatic day because the boat seemed to be
rocking for no reason at all.

Then she lifted her head with a sigh and climbed
up into the main cabin and bent down to pick up
her bag. Only something impinged on her field of
vision and she straightened incredulously and with
her heart pounding.

'*You*,' she whispered. 'But . . . they said they
were keeping you in for the night . . .'

Guy Richardson straightened up. He'd been
leaning against the cabin doorway as if he'd
watched her every move from the moment she'd
hoisted her bag up the steps. He looked pale
beneath his tan, she thought, and tired and he was
dressed more formally than she'd ever seen him in
a pair of white linen trousers and a dark blue shirt
that matched his eyes. But it was his eyes that
shocked her as much as his being there because the
expression in them was coldly cynical and angry.

He said, 'They tried to tell me that too. Only
there's nothing wrong with me . . . and I had the
queer idea that you would take the opportunity to
run away, Leonie. It seems I wasn't wrong.' He
looked her over contemptuously so that she felt
curiously shrivelled and guilty.

She licked her lips. 'I'm not running away,'
she said with difficulty. 'I'm . . . putting an end
to something that was . . . misguided and foolish
in the first place. For which I take full
responsibility and this . . . seemed to be the best
way to do it.'

'Then you left it too late,' he said softly but with

his eyes glittering with so much menace that she swallowed and had to forcibly prevent herself from stepping backwards fearfully.

'Much too late,' he said and although he made no move towards her, he saw the sudden clenching of her fists, and smiled slightly. Which frightened her more, somehow.

'Why?' she whispered. 'Nothing has . . .'

'Oh, but it has happened. In fact exactly what you planned has happened, my dear. You've hooked me like a fish on a line. The only thing I'm not too sure about is *why* you planned to do this but after all, that's only a detail . . . I want you, Leonie. And I'm going to have you . . .'

'No . . .'

'Yes.'

She closed her eyes briefly and tried desperately to concentrate, and to control the insidious trembling of her limbs. 'You . . . the way you're looking at me now makes me think that you hate and despise me rather than . . . anything else.'

'Looks can be deceptive, then,' he murmured.

'All the same . . .'

'All the same,' he acknowledged with irony, 'do I . . . *like* you—is that what you were going to say? To be honest, I don't know. But it doesn't seem to matter. I told you, it's too late now . . .'

She moved convulsively and looked around desperately but of course there was no escape.

'Oh,' he said with a lethal kind of gentleness and came forward but only to pick up her bag, 'not right here, not right now, so don't try to cast yourself overboard, my dear, but finish the week you offered me we will, only with a change of location. And in the days we've got left we might find out a few surprising facts. For example, that it can also happen to *you* . . . this curious business of wanting someone you don't particularly like . . .'

'Please,' she said shakily, 'I *know* I I . . . that it was a stupid thing to do . . .'

'You can tell me all about it later. Who cleaned up here?' he added abruptly.

'I did . . . Guy . . .'

'You're a strange girl, Leonie,' he said with a shrug. 'That's another thing, I believe you saved my life. Now don't think I'm not grateful but I have to confess that as well as gratitude, the thought of it has awoken a queer emotion within me. It seems to put you one up on me. And I'm just a little tired of you being in that position, let's say.'

'I'm *not* . . . I didn't anyway. Who told you that?'

'That you'd saved my life? The same person who told me to expect a bit of a mess on the *Marie-Claire* and that he'd brought you here . . .'

'Not . . . Bill?' she whispered.

'The same. I rang him at his home when there was no sign of you, or anyone for that matter at the hospital to fill me in on about a third of a day I seemed to have lost track of . . . He'd just arrived home. Ready?' he said curtly.

'Where are we going . . . *no* . . .'

He grasped her arm in a grip that wouldn't be broken. 'Home,' he said. 'My place . . . Don't fight me, Leonie,' he warned, 'because it might just make me lose my temper and work out some plan to kidnap you. Which, at this point in time, I'd have no qualms about whatsoever.'

She looked into his eyes and believed him . . .

The trip in the silver Rolls Royce was accomplished in silence. In truth, Leonie felt too exhausted and

dazed to fully comprehend what was happening to
her. It seemed like a dark dream and all she could
think coherently was that she should never have
expended the time and the last reserves of her
energy, that had been over-taxed anyway by the
events of the morning, on cleaning up the *Marie-
Claire*. Because if she hadn't done that, she might
not now be in quite such a state of petrified and
somehow boneless paralysis . . .

Home proved to be a luxury unit in a high-rise
block facing the beach at Surfer's Paradise. It was
exquisitely furnished in pale pastels and subdued,
foil wallpapers and the view from the wide
windows that led on to a terrace was a breath-
taking vision of the lights of Surfer's and further
down the coast against a backdrop of midnight
blue sky.

But Leonie only glanced at the view briefly and
turned away to stand with her head bent and her
arms hanging numbly at her sides.

'What is it?' he said and came back from
switching on lamps and adjusting the curtains, to
tilt her chin up with his fingers.

She didn't even try to veil her eyes, she seemed
to be just too tired and drained to care.

And perhaps he saw it as he studied the dark
shadows like bruises beneath her eyes and the way
her lips weren't quite steady. For he said with a
curious roughness, 'What you need is a long, hot
bath, and bed.'

'I'm clean . . .'

'You may be but you're also as taut as a piano-
wire. And I suspect we're both going to be a bit
stiff tomorrow. A warm soak might help. Come.'
He took her hand.

She didn't resist except for an instant when he

opened a bedroom door and she tensed and thought, please, not Claire's room again . . .

But if it was Claire's bedroom there was no indication of it. It just looked like a spare bedroom with a single bed in it, decorated in pink and grey.

And she sat down on the bed while he disappeared through another doorway and she heard a bath being run, and thought about getting her night clothes out of her bag that he'd put on the floor, but couldn't translate the thought into a deed.

He did it for her, leaving a pile of clothes on the floor. And he took her hand and drew her to her feet and led her into the bathroom which was filled with steam.

'I . . . I can manage now, thanks,' she whispered, making what seemed like an incredible effort.

'All right,' He handed her her robe and nightgown. 'Perhaps you oughtn't to stay too long,' he added abruptly. 'You might fall asleep.'

But she didn't fall asleep in the bath. In fact as she got out and dried herself finally and slipped on her grey silk nightgown and lilac robe, she wondered if she'd gone past the stage of falling asleep, or if her mind had flickered like a trip-switch and she was really asleep but didn't know it . . .

She walked back into the bedroom and looked at the bed and then lay down on it, on top of the cover and with her robe still on but with her eyes open.

'Leonie?'

She turned her head.

He was standing beside the bed with a glass in his hand. 'Have some of this. You look as if you need it.'

'Brandy again?' she whispered.

'Yes . . . drink it all.'

She did, obediently, then started to lie back but he stopped her and helped her to take her robe off and he pulled back the covers and the sheet. 'Get in,' he said quietly and pulled the sheet up when she had. 'Do you think you're going to be able to sleep?'

But perhaps the brandy had done the trick because as she turned her cheek to the pillow her eyelids grew heavy and she thought, I'm not asleep after all . . . I can close my eyes . . .

And she felt sleep claiming her, pulling her down into a welcome, hazy place that was warm and soft and above all, blank . . .

CHAPTER FIVE

IT was sunlight that brought her back to consciousness. Filtered sunlight streaming through a thin, gauzy patch of cloud and when she got up and looked out of the window it was to see that the day could go either way.

There were patches of sunlight out to sea too, and a streak of clear blue sky on the horizon but when she looked towards the mountains behind the coast she saw ridges of grey, purplish cloud building up.

Not that the vagaries of the weather were daunting the early morning surfers riding the swells on their boards and looking small and toy-like from the twentieth floor.

She watched for a while then turned away from the window with a sigh.

True to Guy Richardson's prediction she felt a bit stiff physically but that was nothing compared to her over-burdened state of mind. Not even a deep and dreamless sleep had cured that.

So what am I going to do? she asked herself as she dressed once more in her jeans and blue shirt. Perhaps the only thing I can do is tell him the truth now. Surely that will . . . resolve the issue. He couldn't still want me once he knows. Unless he decides to take revenge . . .

She shivered involuntarily at the thought. Or perhaps my best hope is to try to . . . slip away again. After all he can't keep me a prisoner here, can he?

She bit her lip and rested her brush as she recalled the look in his eyes when he'd threatened to kidnap her yesterday.

'I wouldn't put it past him,' she whispered. 'And perhaps the time to try and escape is right now when it's still very early—he might even be still asleep.'

Yes, that's it, she thought, the element of surprise . . . He probably expects me to sleep in . . .

And she began to re-pack her bag with a sort of feverish haste but as quietly as possible and looking cautiously, every now and then, at the closed door.

But all of a sudden she stopped and lifted her head as if struck by a sudden thought. The bag had been empty when she'd picked it up except for the two paperbacks . . .

She emptied it again, methodically. Then she picked it up and turned it upside down, turned it inside out, all the time with her eyes narrowed as if in an effort to concentrate.

She put it down finally and glanced around the room, taking in every surface but there was nothing . . .

'*You* bastard,' she whispered and stalked to the door to fling it open.

There was no sign of Guy Richardson in the lounge or kitchen but he appeared after only five minutes during which she'd paced up and down the lounge-dining-room area like a caged tiger, but not quietly.

'Leonie?' he said, looking at her with his eyebrows raised beneath his still tousled hair. He only wore a pair of jeans and was unshaven—in fact he looked so exactly like he had the first time she'd laid eyes on him, it incensed her even more for some reason.

'Give them back to me,' she spat at him. 'My wallet and my bank book. You had no right to . . . to steal them from me. Just as you have no right to keep me here like a prisoner with not a cent to my name . . .'

'I didn't steal them precisely,' he murmured. 'I merely removed them just in case you woke up early and tried to run away again.' His lips twitched. 'I really have no designs on your money, Leonie. As for being a prisoner, why don't you think of yourself as a prisoner of love? Doesn't that sound . . . romantic?' he queried, his eyes patiently amused.

'*Oh* . . .' She ground her teeth and her eyes flashed brilliantly and furiously.

'You're lovely at the best of times, my dear,' he drawled, 'but you're magnificent when you're in a temper.'

That did it. She launched herself at him with every intention of scratching his eyes out but he only laughed and caught her wrists in one hand, in a merciless, crushing grip and with his other hand on her shoulder forced her on to her knees on the carpet in front of him.

She closed her eyes, silently vowing not to give him the satisfaction of seeing that he was hurting her, not to mention humiliating her. But while the defiance was there when she opened them again to stare up at him, it was mingled with fear, something she couldn't hide.

They stayed like that for perhaps a minute. Then he swore suddenly beneath his breath and released her wrists only to kneel down beside her as she crumpled slightly and take her into his arms.

'Don't look like that . . .' he said in a curiously husky voice. 'I'm sorry.'

Leonie took a breath but to her horror and despair, it didn't stop the hot tears from welling and coursing down her cheeks.

Then, she didn't quite know how he achieved it, but they were sitting on the floor, she partly in his lap and he was leaning back against a chair.

He let her cry for a while, just stroking her hair. And when the tears began to subside and she moved convulsively, as if bitterly conscious that the last thing she should have done was weep into his shoulder of all things, he said quite normally, 'I don't know about you but I'm useless at this time of day before I've had a cup of tea. Would you like one?'

She stared at him then could only nod helplessly.

'Right.' He got up and picked her up and put her down in a chair. 'I'll get it.'

But before he went, he turned on a lamp because that early sunlight had disappeared and it had started to rain heavily.

It took him about ten minutes because, she saw, he'd shaved and showered, too. And it was a tray of tea and toast he set on a small table he'd drawn up beside her chair. He sat down himself on the other side of the table. And when she opened her mouth to say something he just shook his head slightly and motioned for her to drink her tea.

It was hot and sweet and the toast buttered and spread with marmalade. Finally, when she'd eaten a slice and drunk her tea, he poured her another cup and got up and fetched a napkin from the dining area to wipe her fingers on.

Then he picked up his refilled cup and went to stand at the terrace windows with it. He stared out at the rain-swept sea for several moments.

Until finally he turned back to her and said abruptly, 'Leonie, as much for your own sake as anything else, I think you owe me an explanation. I never totally accepted the one you gave me, and less than ever now. But I can't,' he shrugged, 'perhaps don't want to ... believe the obvious one that springs to mind.' He looked down at the cup in his hand and then directly at her, his eyes dark and brooding. '*Did* you ... scrape an acquaintance with me with some idea of marrying me one day? And then got cold feet?'

Leonie took a quivering breath and knew that the only thing she could do now was tell him the truth ...

'No,' she said in a low voice. 'No ...'

'Then what was the motive behind it all? There was one, wasn't there?'

She looked up then swiftly down again. 'Yes. Revenge ...'

He made an incredulous gesture. 'But you and I had never met. That doesn't make sense! Unless you've got some crazy thing against men ...'

The nails of her left hand, hidden in her lap, bit into her palm but she said as evenly as she could, 'Not men in general. What ... I resented about you, is not something confined to men. Nor was it on my behalf. It was for my sister ...'

. She raised her head again and her grey eyes were bleak and bitter. 'You ... destroyed her. Her life, her marriage ...'

He stared at her with his eyes narrowed as if racking his brains for some resemblance that had escaped him and the only sound was the rain beating and hissing against the concrete floor of the terrace.

'Anne Walker,' she said. 'Does that name ring a bell?'

His mouth hardened then, and his eyes went cold. 'Oh, yes,' he said after a moment and put his cup down with something of a click. 'Yes, indeed. So Anne's your sister? I'd never have guessed it. But you've ...' He stopped and tilted his head to one side. 'Well, we'll get to that later. How did you plan to get this revenge, on your sister's behalf, of course?' he asked ironically.

'I ...' her voice cracked a little, 'planned to try and make you fall in love with me ... and then I was going to turn you down, flat ... walk away from you as you did to her ...'

Her voice wound down to barely above a whisper and she lifted her hands to her face suddenly and thought, Oh God, *saying* it makes it sound cheap and ... horrible. It's the first time I've actually said it out loud ... I've only thought it ever since that day in the music block at St Bede's when Claire Richardson began to talk about her father and the seeds of this plan began to germinate in my mind.

She took her hands from her face abruptly and there were fresh tears in her eyes as she said huskily, 'It was a stupid, foolish thing to do ... to think I could do. I began to see that gradually. That's why ...' But she found she couldn't go on and shrugged helplessly.

'Does that mean you've found out something that acquits me of ruining your sister's life?'

'No,' she whispered, 'it's not that, although ...'

'Go on, Leonie,' he said finally.

'I ... just found myself feeling *cheap*. Especially,' she took a breath, 'as I know your daughter.' There, it's out she thought. Surely the one thing

that will make him hope to God he never lays eyes
on me again. But besides that, he's going to find it
out someday . . .

She closed her eyes briefly, then looked at him
still with tears shimmering in them, but unflinchingly. 'I teach her music.'

She saw the shock in his eyes and looked away.

'Does . . . Claire know anything about this?' he
demanded.

'Oh no!' She turned back to him urgently.

'Forgive me,' he said harshly, 'but in the face of
all the rest of this it wouldn't be hard to disbelieve
you. If nothing else you must have . . . so *she* was
the source of all your carefully done homework!'
he said violently.

'Yes, but not because I . . . pumped her . . .'

'Oh, come on! Am I supposed to believe that?
What the hell do you take me for? But then I
ought to know that, I suppose.'

'Then you don't know very much,' Leonie
retorted suddenly angry herself. 'Yes, I did learn
about you from Claire, I admit that. But not
because I ever asked her or even encouraged her.
Because that's one thing she needs no en-
couragement to talk about . . . you. You have one
. . . great fan . . . oh *hell*,' she said herself. 'All
right, I feel guilty about Claire although I never
. . . never had any intention of her knowing about
this, let alone playing any part in it. And if you
were to ask anyone at St Bede's they would tell
you—be able to tell you everything *I* know about
you. She adores you and she talks about you and
your boats, everything about you . . .'

They stared at each other.

'And,' Leonie said after an age, 'if we're to
measure up guilt—because I found I couldn't go

through with this, doesn't lessen *your* guilt. It only, if the truth be known, highlights the fact that I found I had some scruples I didn't know I possessed.'

'Later, I'd like to dispute that,' he said with an effort, as if he was so angry he found it hard to speak. 'But in the meantime, tell me about your sister Anne and what I'm supposed to have done to ruin her life and marriage, Leonie. Tell me all about it.'

She hesitated. 'You took her up and dropped her. What more is there to tell?'

He laughed. '*I* took her up? No, *she* too me up, your sister Anne. And the only thing I ever did to her was forcibly prevent her from throwing herself into the Broadwater one night, and taking her to someone for help.'

'That's not *true*,' Leonie whispered.

'But it is. And I have witnesses. Didn't you *know* what she was like?'

'I know she was my baby sister . . . I . . . she told me all about you.'

'Your *baby* sister,' he said ironically. 'If anyone had asked me, I'd have said she was born knowing it all. As for that wimp she was married to . . . But of course, it was your sister you were talking about yesterday, who gave up everything for another man, then found she had nothing. No wonder Laurel confused you.' His tone was contemptuous.

'Not about this, she didn't,' Leonie said quietly. 'Nor did I expect you to admit it.'

'I admit nothing. I . . .' His voice changed suddenly from a tone of violent impatience to something more dangerous, perhaps. 'But where were you when all this was going on? Were you here? A silent witness?' His eyes challenged her.

'. . . No.'

'I thought not,' he said sardonically. 'Just as a matter of interest though, where were you?'

'I . . . I was in Papua New Guinea.'

'Were you now,' he said mockingly. 'I might have known it would be somewhere different. What were you doing up there? Teaching music to the Kuka Kukas? Or being a journalist photographer . . . no, don't tell me. You were up there championing whatever is the local, popular cause of the moment.'

Her lips tightened. 'None of those. Nor do I propose to tell you . . .'

'Then let's gets back to your sister,' he said harshly. 'Tell me more about her—your side of the story.'

Their eyes clashed. 'It's not *my* side of the story, but if I thought you would believe one word I said, I would,' she answered angrily.

'And if you thought it would be your key to getting out of here?' he asked negligently, leaning his shoulders against the wall.

She looked around. 'You *can't* keep me here against my will.'

'I could certainly try . . .'

She swallowed then said abruptly, 'All right, what do you want to know?'

'What she was like as a child. Let's start with that.'

Leonie looked at him steadily. 'If you're trying to make me admit she had some kind of a . . . a character flaw . . .'

'You're damn right I am,' he interrupted.

'To ease your conscience,' she went on deliberately, 'she didn't. She was a little more highly strung than I was and . . .' Leonie stopped and flushed slightly.

'Go on,' he prompted. 'A little more used to getting her own way as the baby of the family than you were? In fact quite a spoilt, petulant little girl and your mother's favourite,' he said flatly but his eyes were piercingly acute.

'No ...' she whispered and stared up at him. 'How did you know ...?' She bit her lip and looked away with suddenly anguished eyes.

'I'll tell you in a minute. But why do you delude yourself about it?'

'I ... it wasn't quite like that,' she said very quietly 'If Anne was my mother's favourite it was because she took after her while I was very like my father. I told you what he did so I suppose I was like a constant reminder to my mother of something she was trying to forget.'

'Hardly fair to you,' he commented. 'Or to Anne for that matter. Because she grew up to be very used to getting her own way which explains a lot about her.'

Leonie stood up and began to pace around agitatedly. '*What* does it explain? If you're trying to say Anne became a ... an alcoholic nymphomaniac on the strength of that there's no doubt you're a better boat-builder than a psychiatrist! When I left for Papua New Guinea, she and Ron had been married for six months, *happily*. She'd got over our mother's death and—well, you only had to look at her to know she was happy. But when I came back she'd changed out of all recognition. And all because of you, she said ...'

'Did you get any details?'

'Of course! They left Townsville because Ron couldn't get work and when they arrived on the Coast he applied to you for a job which he got.

Anne really met you for the first time at a works'
Christmas party, she said. You paid her a lot of
attention and afterwards you ... pestered her in
fact. She was working, too, and because they only
had one car, she used to drop Ron off in the
mornings and pick him up in the evenings. And
when she had to wait for him some evenings you
used the opportunity to chat her up ...'

·'And you believe that—now?' he shot at her.

'I ...' Leonie hesitated, 'she was the most
beautiful girl I've ever seen,' she said simply.

'Was?' he queried.

'Well, she's a little ... frayed around the edges
now.'

'Where is she?'

'In Sydney. She and Ron are back together but
it's a horrible kind of relationship now. Everything
they say to each other is loaded and every word
seems to have a double meaning—it's as if all they
want to do is hurt each other ... It reminded me
of the way my mother and father were before he
moved out. She, too, my mother, used to get a sort
of twisted pleasure out of sitting in righteous
judgment on my father. Ron is the same ...'

'He was as much to blame as anyone.'

'How ...? Not that I'm accepting this ...'

'You will,' Guy Richardson say drily. 'You see,
they were both ... restless by then but incredibly
naïve. They were both seeking new horizons—
possibly because they were too bloody young to be
married in the first place. And you're right, if you
liked mindless loveliness, your sister Anne was the
epitome of it. Ron used that, they both used it as
an entrée to the kind of people he met coming
through my boat yard. People he thought
represented the world and didn't realise for the

Peggy had said wisely. 'Perhaps the seeds were always there and it only needed the right circumstances to make them flourish. She had, you both had, an unstable childhood but whereas you were able to cope with it, she wasn't. I think, too, you were perhaps forced to stand on your own two feet quite young which she wasn't, then found she couldn't ... She seemed to me to be the kind of person who constantly needed to be reassured that she was loved. You see what we often mistake for tantrums, perhaps thinking someone has been spoiled by the way they act, are in fact just that, cries for reassurance. Then, too, she married someone who I believe was as uncertain in his own way as she was and not the person who could be like the rock she needed.'

'He ... I don't suppose he was,' Leonie had said slowly. 'But they were ... they looked to be so much in love.'

'Those kind of inner deficiencies put great strains on love, my dear,' Peggy had said gently. 'Other things, too. Both of them got a glimpse of a world that was a far cry from the kind of lifestyle they could afford and that undoubtedly chafed them both. We mustn't forget they were very young. How is Anne now?' she'd asked then. 'I was in two minds when they left the coast. I knew they had to make some kind of a break and try to start again but I really felt I was getting through to her so ...' She's shrugged unhappily.

'I haven't seen her for months, although I write every week. But the last time I saw her ...'

'Was she drinking?'

'No ... But she might just as well have been. It's as if she's lost interest in everything, even herself, her looks ... And all the time Ron is gibing at her and she at him. I should have asked him about it all,' Leonie said miserably. 'But the veiled sort of comments he made from time to time seemed to fit in with her story. I still ... why did she lie to me?'

'My dear,' Peggy had said, 'you must realise that she lied to *herself* about Guy. That was one of my big problems with her. She used to say to me, "I know he loves me, too, but he won't do anything about it because I'm married". Oh, yes,' she'd said to Leonie's look of shock. And gone on, 'But I had thought I'd got her to understand that she was fooling herself, that it was a sort of defence mechanism she was using. I really did think she'd admitted that, finally. Perhaps you were the one person who she just couldn't bear to know that she'd made such a fool of herself, such a mess of her life without cause. You know, she didn't ever say much to me about you, just that she had an older sister but she did say, several times, if only I was more like her ...'

'Oh, God,' Leonie said after a long time.

'My dear, are you all right?' Peggy had asked concernedly.

'Oh ... yes,' Leonie had answered as if coming out of an unpleasant reverie. And had added with an effort, 'It's just to think that all these months I've ...' She stopped abruptly.

Peggy had hesitated. Then she'd said tentatively, 'Guy is possibly upset that you would have thought that of him but once you've explained ...'

'Yes,' Leonie had said with an effort and an inward shiver. Only you don't know how I went about it all, Peggy, she thought, although you must suspect now ...

'Would you like me to come up with you?' Peggy's voice had cut into her thoughts.

'No . . . No thank you, Peggy. I . . . it will be all right. Anyway, I owe you a great debt as it is, for all you did for Anne. I'm really grateful.'

Guy had been on the 'phone when she'd got back upstairs. He'd let her in and motioned her into the lounge and gone back to what sounded like a business call.

Not that Leonie took much of it in. She was still too dazed and stunned by all that she'd learnt this morning and the implications of it to be able to take much in at all. But finally she heard the receiver go down and footsteps and she swallowed and licked her lips and forced herself to look up . . .

'I don't know what to say.' Her voice was husky and uneven but she forced herself to go on. 'I can only tell you that I feel awful for allowing myself to make an error of judgment like that about you, especially when you probably saved her life. I should have checked her story out but I just had no cause to disbelieve her. I *should* have asked Ron what really happened but he made it rather obvious that he didn't appreciate me butting in. The whole situation was horribly awkward and I felt so helpless. All the same I don't usually . . . I'm not usually prone to rash acts but . . .' She stopped and sighed.

'But you do have a record of . . . taking action about things you feel strongly about,' Guy Richardson said with a tinge of irony. 'Your article on Moreton Island, for example.'

'Well, yes. That must be it,' she said tremulously.

'I wonder,' he murmured and cast himself down in a chair and regarded her silently for a time.

Until she said uncertainly, 'What?'

'My dear Leonie,' he said, 'at our first meeting you rather successfully passed yourself off as someone confident and experienced—with men, someone well able to look after themselves. Even so, it was an enormous gamble you took, especially if you cherished the kind of thoughts about me you did. But then, little by little, I began to wonder just how experienced you were. Sometimes you seemed even a bit frightened of me and I began to wonder if it hadn't all been an act. I still don't really know . . . and that bothers me, you see.'

'Why?' she whispered.

'Because if it was all an act, I can't believe that even your sister's plight—what you thought had happened to Anne—would be enough to . . . put yourself at risk like that. I think there would have to have been an ulterior motive, too.'

'Like what?'

He stared at her. 'I don't know,' he said after a while. 'But I aim to find out.'

She found herself thinking that his last words had a curious quality about them, like the clanging shut of a prison door. And she felt a beading of sweat spring to her forehead. 'Then,' she said dully, 'you're not going to . . . forgive me.'

'I wouldn't say that. Look upon it more as a challenge, if you like. In other words come clean with me, Leonie. At least have the guts to do that.'

'I don't know what you're talking about. I had no ulterior motive . . .' She sprang up agitatedly.

But all he said, mildly, was, 'If you insist. But,' he sat up and his eyes were suddenly piercingly intent and his mouth hard, 'you had a motive for trying to get out of this *before* you found out the truth, didn't you? What was that?'

'I told you . . .'

'You told me you felt cheap. Did you not also feel that the relationship you started with me so cold-bloodedly was getting a little out of hand, Leonie? A little less than cold-blooded, perhaps?' he said sardonically.

A spasm of something like fear crossed her features and she turned away quickly to hide it but perhaps not quickly enough for he laughed softly, unpleasantly.

'*That's* what I mean,' he said, 'about coming clean with me, my dear. Forget about the rest of it now and how it all started, just have the courage to acknowledge that something . . . flowered out of it all for you as well as me, however unexpected. And let us go on from there.'

Leonie stood with her head bent, trying to think. Finally she turned to look at him and said, 'Do I have a choice?'

He held her eyes with his and she knew she'd said the wrong thing as she saw a bright flame of anger begin to turn in the deep blue of his eyes. 'Put it this way,' he said drily, 'you have the choice of being co-operative or uncooperative. If you choose the latter . . .'

'You can't force me to . . . to do anything,' she said with her heart beating hurriedly and her mouth suddenly dry.

'If I was so minded there's not a lot you could do about anything I might force upon you. You don't seem to understand that. However, I think I'd rather be more subtle about it. I don't know how dear you hold your job but it would only take a few words from me to ensure that you lost it and not only that, never got another one like it. In other words you would be black-listed. You may never have intended to involve Claire, I don't believe you did—at least I don't *think* you did, but without uttering one word of a lie, I could paint a very odd picture of you to your headmistress. I could also get in touch with the editor of the magazine that published your article on sand-mining and let him know just what unscrupulous methods you tried to use to get a story on me ... It's up to you now to consider if it's worth going through all that. For a lost cause,' he added.

She felt the heat stealing into her cheeks as he unconsciously echoed her earlier thoughts on the subject. Oh God, she thought, I must have been mad to let myself get trapped into this whole thing in the first place. Why did I? *Why* ... Is he right about an ulterior motive? Is it because of ... other things that I felt so burningly resentful and angry about what happened, what I thought happened to Anne?

She rubbed her face wearily and said finally in a low voice, 'I can understand you being angry and wanting to extract some kind of ... counter-revenge for what I did. But to cloak it with something else ...'

'If that's what you think, you don't understand at all,' he interrupted tightly.

'We've only known each other for four days!' she said desperately.

'A hell of a lot can happen in four days,' he retorted. 'But for that matter, I was intrigued about you after about four minutes. And nothing that's happened since has altered that. I told you last night how it was ...'

'I still think it's a kind of revenge,' she whispered.

'Then think that if it makes you happy.' His
eyes glittered. 'But—as I said once before—come
hell or high water I want you, Leonie. And I *don't*
believe you're entirely unaffected by me, only that
you won't admit it. And that's what riles me.
Look, if you hated me, what were you going to do
when I wouldn't be fobbed off? Were you going to
fake a reaction to my kisses, my embraces?'

'I . . .' She closed her eyes.

'You were, weren't you? Then you found you
couldn't, didn't you? In fact you got so carried
away kissing me, it took about a hundred
whistling, cat-calling people to bring you back.
And that's when you thought of getting out! Look
at me, Leonie!' he commanded.

She did and he went on with a chilling kind of
menace, 'Curiously, the fact that you won't admit
it upsets me far more than all the other deceptions
you practised on me. Perhaps a man can only
stand being made a fool of up to a point,' he said
with a sort of twisted irony. 'Perhaps I am trying
to take revenge, but for *that*. Now do you
understand?' He got up and walked over to her
and his expression was so grim, she tried to back
away but a chair was behind her.

'Do you, Leonie?' he repeated.

She nodded dumbly, fighting back tears again.

'Then what are we going to do about it? It's
your choice.'

The tears that she was battling clogged her
throat and made it hard to speak. 'I . . . do admit
it,' she said barely audibly but at the same time
made a gesture of futility with her hands. 'But . . .
it was only a kiss.'

He studied her for a long time. Then he smiled,
a cool movement of his lips that didn't reach his

eyes. 'You don't give up easily, do you, Leonie?
All right, let me put it into the terms you obviously
see it. How are you going to pay for that kiss? By
losing your job, maybe a lot more? Or by letting
me try to show that what's in a kiss,' he raised his
eyebrows mockingly, 'can sometimes go much
deeper than you'd imagine. What did they say
about Helen of Troy—that her face launched a
thousand ships? Speaking nautically, not in-
appropriately,' he grimaced, 'you obviously had
no idea what you were launching when you kissed
me, or, for that matter, when you first looked at
me with those lovely grey eyes. I'm sorry, but
that's the way it is . . . and you don't have to look
so frightened. It's not that I want to hurt you,
quite the opposite. But I'm afraid there's just no
turning me back from this course *you* set . . .'

He lifted a hand and touched her face, her
mouth, her wet cheeks.

'Guy . . .' she whispered on a breath, her eyes
imploring.

But he only said, 'Let's try it again . . .' And
covered her mouth with his.

CHAPTER SIX

THREE days later Leonie looked down at her hands and knew that tonight was the night.

She was sitting at the dressing-table in the pink-and-grey spare room of Guy Richardson's unit high above Surfer's Paradise, dressed in her white crêpe dress and wearing the high-heeled gold mules she'd bought to go with it. And she was brushing her hair . . . until she put the brush down impatiently and stood up . . .

I seem to spend my life agonising in front of mirrors lately, she thought.

They were going out to dinner—she glanced at her watch—in about half and hour, he'd said. She was ready early, not that he was to know that, she mused. The bedroom door was closed. So perhaps I can take the time to think . . .

Yet as she stood in front of the window looking out at the lights with her arms crossed in front of her and her hands cupping her upper arms, all she could think of was the past three days, three days that had led with gentleness, some laughter but all the same with the inevitability of an iron fist in a velvet glove to what was coming tonight, she knew.

Oh, he's been clever about it, she thought. He's never pressed me past that point which he seems to know about instinctively, the point where *I* know I'm going to panic. But I can't expect this to go on for ever. Nor have I exactly repulsed him . . .

She closed her eyes and felt a tremor go through

her as, like cameos, little scenes from the preceding
days flooded her mind and caused her to feel weak
and breathless all over again.

The first time it had happened had been when
he'd kissed her for the second time. She'd stood
mute and shaking in his arms, hemmed in
literally and mentally. Unable to fight him
physically and still too dazed by all she'd learnt
that morning.

And she'd let him kiss her as he pleased. Her
lips, her throat, her hair. Nor had she resisted
when he'd picked her up in his arms and sat down
with her in his lap. But gradually the delicacy and
the warmth of what he was doing to her, the way
his hands moved on her body through the thin silk
of her shirt, had had a curious effect. She'd
thought at the time that any kind of comfort
would have soothed her somewhat, she certainly
was in need of it because she felt as if the world
had crashed around her . . .

But then she found herself not only lulled and
soothed out of that desperate, shaking void she
seemed to have been inhabiting, but actually
responding to him. Her lips had parted beneath his
and even the knowledge that what she was doing
further eroded her, at best, flimsy defence, had not
stopped her.

Although, when it had finished finally and she'd
lain against him with her body trembling but in an
entirely new way, she'd been unable to hide the
vulnerable expression in her eyes, as if she was
expecting him to say—I told you so . . .

But he'd surprised her. He'd touched her mouth
with his fingers and said, although huskily, 'How
about a swim?'

'. . . It's raining.'

'No. It's stopped. The sun's out. And the surf will be good . . .'

The surf had been good, not too rough but invigorating and they'd stayed in for about an hour, catching waves and planing towards the shore to lie breathless in the shallows for a few minutes, then to swim back out.

She'd thought, too, it was exactly what she needed. As if the buffeting the refreshing salt water was giving her body was achieving something for her mind as well, planing away the tensions and confusions and laying it bare to cope with what lay ahead. Because when Guy Richardson had stopped kissing her, she'd known then how right he'd been all along. The real enemy was within herself, that part of her that *was* undoubtedly attracted to him. And she'd known, too, that it was a weapon he was going to use, although she hadn't known then how cleverly he would do it. That knowledge came more slowly.

But there's one thing he doesn't know about me, she'd reflected when they'd finally dried off and walked back across the road to the unit. Because that's my secret. The one thing no-one knows . . . now. My one . . . strength I suppose you could say. But she'd closed her eyes briefly at the thought of it.

It had been later that same day that she'd started to understand just what kind of a subtle campaign Guy Richardson was mounting . . .

They'd not been back at the unit long when the 'phone had rung. He'd spoken into it briefly then turned to her.

'I have to go out. Something's come up at the factory with a new boat we're launching. If they didn't know I was back they'd cope, no doubt . . .

I don't know how long I'll be gone. Will you be all right?'

'Yes . . .'

'Have some lunch. There's plenty of stuff in the fridge. We never did get around to breakfast.' And he'd bent his head and kissed her briefly, then was gone.

It was she who touched her lips this time and stood staring into space for quite a while after the front door had closed.

Then, feeling curiously unclean, she'd started to search the unit for her wallet and bank book but had not found them and known then that he'd locked them away in the beautiful mahogany desk in the study-cum-den, the only thing she found she couldn't get into . . .

And she'd shrugged and thought that anyway, if she had escaped he would know where to find her. And she'd made herself a sandwich and a cup of tea and taken it back to the den.

There was plenty of evidence of Claire in that room. A framed photo of her on top of the piano, a bookcase full of books that would appeal to a twelve-year-old and a squash racquet that bore her name on the cover.

Leonie had sat down at the piano but in the end not lifted the lid. Instead, she'd got up and turned on the television and rearranged a pile of cushions left on the floor as if someone made a practice of watching television in that position.

But once lying down comfortably herself, her eyelids had drooped and she'd fallen asleep.

Hours later she'd been woken slowly by someone just stroking her bare shoulder and arm gently.

'Mmmm,' she'd murmured sleepily and moved

her shoulder luxuriously. Then the hand had
stopped and she'd sighed and turned on to her
back, to find herself staring up into Guy
Richardson's dark blue, amused eyes.

'Oh!' She'd sat up guiltily. 'I . . . what time is it?'
Not that late, surely!'

But the darkening sky outside had confirmed
the time on his watch.

'Does it matter?' he'd enquired with his lips
twitching.

'No. . . I suppose not.'

'Anyway you've had yesterday to get over—as
well as today. Two difficult days in a variety of
ways.'

She'd said nothing, only looked at him
uncertainly, wondering what to expect next. And
he'd surprised her again.

'What are your favourite movies? Got any?'

She'd frowned. '*Oliver—The Sound of Music* . . .
Well, I guess they're hangovers from my childhood
but they seem to be the ones that spring to mind.
Although, that's not quite true. I love good
musicals.'

'Right. So do I, as a matter of fact. I'll see if I
can get one or the other.'

'How?' she'd asked curiously.

'Well, I've got a video machine and there's a
video library just downstairs. There's also an
Indonesian restaurant downstairs that does take-
aways. Their Nassi Goreng is superb. Do you like
that kind of thing?'

'As a matter of fact I adore Nassi Goreng,'
Leonie had said then stopped self-consciously
because it all seemed so natural—two people
planning their evening as if nothing deep and dark
existed between them at all.

Yet that's how it had gone on, the evening, so naturally. The Nassi Goreng had been perfect with the right sambals, banana, coconut and the wine he'd opened had been chilled and refreshing ... and Lionel Bart's music had done the rest.

'I always thought Ron Moody was superb as Fagin,' she'd said a little dreamily when *Oliver* had finished. 'I mean, I know it probably isn't quite how Charles Dickens intended, the movie, because he's my favourite character, him and Dodger,' she'd added ruefully.

Guy had laughed briefly. 'Not what Dickens had in mind,' he'd murmured. 'But I know what you mean. They were both compelling perform-ances. The other thing about it is all the kids. They're so natural but then kids are as actors, aren't they?'

'Well,' she'd said a shade wryly, 'they are when you see them like that but we're putting on a musical at St Bede's next term and ...' She'd stopped and thought, oh God! Why did I bring that up?

But he'd only laughed again and said, 'I know what you mean. I've sat through a few school musicals. Is Claire in it?'

'Yes ... she's rather musical.'

'Then she must have got it from her mother, not from me.'

'You sang the other night quite ...'

'Tunefully?'

'Well, yes.'

'Then that's the extent of it. I can't play anything. How many instruments do you play?'

'Three or four but my favourite is the piano. I once ... quite thought I was good enough to be a concert pianist. But that was when I was very young.'

'Play something for me, Leonie?'

She looked at him. 'Now?'

'Mmmm—if you feel like it,' he'd said lazily and laid his head back.

She'd played for about half an hour, mostly classics, her favourites. Then when she'd wondered if he'd fallen asleep and she'd closed the piano, he'd said, 'Will Claire ever be able to play like that?'

She'd hesitated.

'Don't answer that,' he'd murmured and stood up. 'You're always surprising me, Leonie. Although I don't know why about this. I suppose I didn't expect your playing to give me goose bumps. Claire was right . . .'

Her lips had parted in surprise. 'You mean Claire talked about me?'

'Yes. Only I didn't connect her Miss Powell with you until . . .'

'It was too late,' she had whispered unhappily.

'That remains to be seen, my dear,' he'd replied and drawn her into his arms. 'She was right about one thing, though, Claire. She told me you played the piano beautifully.'

Leonie had shivered.

He'd held her closer and said into her hair, 'Why did you do that?'

'The weight of my sins, perhaps,' she'd answered very quietly.

He'd said nothing for a long time and she had become acutely conscious of the feel of his tall, strong body against her own, of the way he made her feel . . . slight, as he'd once said, but in the slender sense of the word. And vulnerable, too, yet . . . curiously as if that very vulnerability was a key with which to unlock . . . something within him,

something special if only she knew how to use it.
As if it was not a weakness but a strength, *her*
contribution ...

Only, she'd thought then, I don't know how to
use it, I never did and I never learnt. Perhaps it's
just a will o' the wisp anyway, something
mermaids dream about ...

'Would you mind if I kissed you good night?'
His voice had interrupted her thoughts.

'I ...'

But he'd taken possession of her mouth in a way
that was becoming familiar.

And finally he'd lifted his head and said, 'You
don't—mind kissing me, do you?'

She'd only been able stare up at him.

'Well, it's a start. Good night, my dear.' He'd
released her, then taken her hand and led her to
the spare bedroom. 'Sleep well,' he'd murmured,
and closed the door between them.

She had, unexpectedly. Because she'd spent a
long time once in bed staring at the wall opposite,
staring at things her mind had conjured up, scenes
of violence, scenes of ...

Then she'd fallen asleep quite suddenly.

The next day had taken another turn.

'Saw Brad yesterday,' Guy had said over
breakfast. 'He's got a runner at Murwillumbah
today. How would you like to go to the races?'

'Provided I don't have to dress up. I haven't any
special gear ...'

He'd grinned. 'People dress down if anything for
there. It's a little country track ...'

So she'd washed her jeans and pink blouse and
dried them in the drier, and she'd put her hair
up—the first time he'd seen her that way, and put

on a pair of gold hoop earrings. All the make-up
she wore was a glossy pink lipstick and some
mascara because the tan she now had made her
skin glow golden and smooth and she only
moisturised it lightly. The tan even further high-
lighted her luminous grey eyes.

And when she'd stood before him, he'd looked
her up and down and said quietly, 'Gorgeous.
Why don't you bring your camera?'

She'd raised her eyebrows, taken aback for a
moment because in fact she'd been thinking how
nice *he* looked in a pair of cream trousers and a
sage green shirt . . .

'It's very pretty around Murwillumbah and at
the track.'

'All right.'

Murwillumbah was about a twenty-minute drive
inland from Tweed Heads at the southern end of
the Gold Coast, a lovely drive along the banks of
the broad, peaceful Tweed River and between
green cane fields. The town was dominated by two
features, the Condong sugar mill and as a
backdrop to it, the rocky, finger-like Mount
Warning, named by Captain Cook who'd seen it
from the Pacific Ocean. And the racecourse was
situated deep into the cane fields, with its own
bluish purple backdrop of rising hills that formed
the Lamington Plateau.

But apart from the spectacular scenery there'd
been plenty to photograph at the races—Brad's
horse for one thing, a highly excited two-year-old
filly who had had to be dragged into the mounting
yard, had got rid of her jockey before they got on
to the track and then, after playing up terribly
about entering the starting stalls, had left them
cleanly to everyone's amazement and romped in to

win the race by three lengths. The only person not entirely jubilant about her win was the jockey who'd weighed in muttering darkly to himself about getting paid danger money.

Brad, unaccompanied today, had bought a bottle of champagne and asked Leonie humourlessly if he could have copies of the photos she'd taken of all the drama.

Yet far from enjoying herself, Leonie had found quite suddenly as she stood with Brad and Guy in the betting ring later, that the afternoon had gone curiously flat. She'd been unable to put her finger on it as she'd looked around at the colourful throng, at the bookmakers, at the brilliant green lawn that led to the horse stalls—except to feel strangely as if this was some kind of last supper for her. And she'd thought, how can I be enjoying myself? And she'd moved restlessly.

But it had seemed that Guy had noticed even although he was talking to someone, because he'd put out a hand and taken hers. For a moment she'd wanted to resist but had not, although she'd thought rebelliously, how does he do it? See into my mind . . .?

He'd kept her close for the rest of the afternoon, always at her side, often holding her hand so that she'd thought once, ironically, at least we *look* like lovers.

But although she'd wanted to be irritated and resentful at this treatment, in the end it had had the opposite effect . . .

After the last race they'd gone back to the horse stalls with Brad and a man who'd made him an offer for the filly. And she'd stood beside Guy, her hand once more in his but submissively and quietly now and she'd found herself watching him as he and the other two men talked horses, her eyes lingering on the tanned lines of his throat. And she'd thought, I wonder if I were to kiss him there, as he does to me, if it would . . . please him as much as it does me?

Then, to her horror, she'd realised that they'd stopped talking and were all looking at her.

'I . . .' she'd said confusedly, and reached for her sun-glasses on top of her head to mask her eyes. 'What was that?' she'd asked breathlessly.

Brad had laughed. 'Nothing important,' he'd teased and she'd coloured brightly. But Guy hadn't laughed. He'd watched the tide of colour that crept into her cheeks, and she'd got the uncomfortable feeling that he knew exactly what she'd been thinking.

The next day had seen something even more disturbing happen, though. They'd taken the *Marie-Claire* out and he'd shown her more of Moreton Bay and its islands but in the afternoon he'd anchored in a quiet backwater and they'd gone up on to the foredeck to laze off their lunch and sunbathe.

Leonie had smoothed sun-tan lotion all over herself and then leant back against the galley windows with one leg bent up, her face to the sun.

It was incredibly peaceful, being among other things a weekday. And she'd thought he'd fallen asleep stretched out on the deck near her, when there'd been no movement for some time. But when she'd opened her eyes, it was to find that although he lay so still with his head on one arm, he was watching her, his dark blue eyes intent . . .

She'd tensed inwardly and he'd put out a hand and traced the outline of her bent leg. And his touch had sent tremors through her body that she'd not been able to control . . .

'Don't you like that?'

'I . . . yes,' she'd whispered.

'Why don't you take your top off?'

She'd looked down at her bikini top.

'There's no-one about.'

'What for?'

He'd smiled slightly. 'So that I can see your beautiful breasts. They've been tantalising me . . . but I won't touch if you don't want me to.'

She'd lifted her hands and they'd hovered briefly. Then she'd done it, released the little catch and drawn the wisp of silk off but with a sort of defiance, and a challenging glint in her eyes.

'Leonie,' he'd said slowly, his eyes lingering briefly on the paler skin she'd revealed then travelling upwards, 'this is not a war. Put it back on if it makes you happier.'

'You said you wanted to . . .'

'I know . . . I also want to touch them, cup them, feel your nipples hardening beneath my fingers, my lips. The error I made,' his eyes had narrowed, 'was in thinking you might want it, too.'

She'd closed her eyes and tried to steady her breathing which had become curiously erratic. Then she'd opened them and looked downwards with something like despair because just his words had been enough to achieve—just that. Her pink nipples were unfurling, standing up like buds coming into flower and she couldn't prevent herself from visualising his strong brown hands smoothing, stroking, plucking . . .

She'd made a husky, desolate noise in her throat and reached jerkily for her towel but he'd been too quick for her.

'*Why?*' he'd said intently with his hand on her wrist. 'Why do you hate the way I affect you so much? I think I've shown you how much you affect me. I've tried to and I've *told* you . . .'

'Because,' she'd whispered, 'because . . .' She'd stopped and bitten her lip, unable to go on.

'It's not because you're cold . . . I'd lay my life on that. What . . .' He'd stopped then, too, abruptly, as her eyes had flown to his in an unguarded look that had escaped her.

'Oh no, Leonie, it's *not* that,' he'd said through his teeth. 'And I can prove it . . .' He'd sat up swiftly and pulled her glistening almost naked body into his arms.

'Guy . . . you promised,' she'd gasped.

'Some promises are made to be broken, my dear,' he'd answered unevenly.

She'd struggled but to no avail. He'd circled her waist with one arm and held her bent backwards slightly over it and had held her imprisoned with his other hand in her hair. Then he'd lowered his head and begun to kiss her breasts.

She'd held herself taut for as long as she could, but the slow delight he'd inflicted on her had taken hold and her body had been racked by a series of exquisite shudders until she could stand it no more.

She'd said his name on a breath and when he'd lifted his head at last, she'd lifted her arms and slid them around his neck to hold the back of his head in her hands and had stared up at him with tortured eyes.

'Say it, Leonie,' His lips had barely moved. 'Tell me you want me, too. At least tell me that . . .'

'Guy . . .' her lips had quivered, 'all right, I *do* but . . .'

'That's enough,' he'd interrupted suddenly, 'for now.' He'd dropped a light kiss on her hair but she'd felt the taut muscles of his body relax as if he'd forced himself to, and known what kind of an effort it must have cost him, with a sense of guilt.

'Let's have a swim,' he'd gone on to say quite normally although she'd seen a nerve beat in his jaw and found herself wanting to kiss it . . . 'Coming?'

He'd released her and stood up.

She'd stared up at him for a moment, then nodded and held out her hand. He'd pulled her to her feet and handed her her bikini top which she'd turned away to put on. Then they'd climbed down to the back of the boat and dived into the water side by side . . .

And that only happened to me this afternoon, she thought, as she came out of her reverie to find herself still staring at the lights of Surfer's, clad in her white dress and gold mules all ready to go out to dinner.

He's a . . . strange man, she reflected. He could have taken me this afternoon but he held back and I know it wasn't easy. Is that one of the reasons why I know tonight is going to be the night? He said we'd have dinner and dance . . . And anyway, it's going to come to that sooner or later. This is only prolonging the agony for us both . . .

She jumped and turned at a light tap on the door to see it open and Guy standing there dressed in grey trousers and a cream silk shirt, his dark hair brushed and tamed and his eyes apparently bluer.

They said nothing for a moment, just looked at each other assessingly, critically almost. Then he smiled slightly and held out his hand. 'Ready?'

*   *   *

'Is Leonie short for something?'

'In my case, yes. Helen . . .'

'Helen . . . I can't think of you as Helen.'

'I can't remember anyone calling me Helen, except Miss Lucas ... She's the head music teacher at St Bede's.'

'Why did they name you Helen if they always called you Leonie?'

'You'd have to ask them that. But you can't. I think ... perhaps, Helen just doesn't suit a baby somehow, so they looked for a diminutive.'

'Then maybe I should say, Helen, will you let me love you tonight?'

Leonie stopped walking.

It was very late and they'd wined and dined and danced and were now walking along the beach, she with her shoes in one hand, he with his arm about her shoulders.

She was pleasantly tired, the music had been good to dance to and Guy Richardson, like everything else he did apparently, was a good dancer.

And the moon above was waning now but still casting enough light to create shadows on the beach, and the surf was murmuring gently.

She looked out to sea and for a moment the vastness of it captured her. It was after all the Pacific Ocean that stretched all the way to South America and all that lay between were some islands—Norfolk Island, Easter Island, to the south, the Land of the Long White Cloud ... New Zealand, Fiji ... Tahiti ...

'I ... yes,' she said very low, 'if you want to.'

'I want to, perhaps more than you know ...'

She stood still, staring out to sea, then turned and gripped his hand.

*   *   *

'Leonie, the last thing I want to do is hurt you. You're a big girl now—you must know that . . .'

'I do . . .' But she twisted her head on the pillow restlessly. They were both lying naked on a different bed to the one she was used to now—his bed. And the curtains were open so that the reflected lights from Surfer's Paradise were patterned on the wall and the windows were open so that the sound of the sea was there too, dimly. A gentle breeze was floating in.

'Then why are you fighting me?'

She looked around in the darkness with a sigh and found she could picture the room exactly in her mind . . . long aquamarine drapes about the wide windows that brushed the deep silky pile of an oyster wall-to-wall carpet, a peach-pink quilted bedspread that was on the floor now, matching fine percale sheets . . .

She drew up the top sheet. 'Guy . . .'

'Is it that you haven't been quite honest with me, Leonie?' he said very quietly. He wasn't touching her now, just lying on his side with his head propped on one arm, watching her.

'In a way.'

'Are you a virgin? Is *that* it?'

'Oh no,' she whispered with a bitter little smile.

'Then what? We've established that you're not cold—up to a point . . . Has someone taught you to be afraid of this?' He reached out a hand and smoothed the sheet around the curve of her hip and when she couldn't help flinching, he said intently, 'Who was he?'

'I . . .' she hesitated, then she said barely audibly, 'my husband, but it was my fault as much as . . .' Her voice trailed off as she felt him go rigid with shock. 'Guy, he's dead . . . now,' she said urgently. 'He died eighteen months ago in an air crash in New Guinea. I'm not—this is not a repetition of Anne . . . in that respect.'

Guy Richardson rolled over on to his back and lay and said nothing for a time. Then she heard him breath deeply. 'I suspected something like this right at the beginning,' he murmured finally. 'Well, virtually then . . . when you said something about what can happen to you in your own home, your own bedroom. But I got put off that tack somehow—you were so cool . . . Can you talk about it?'

'I'd rather not.'

'Well you're going to whether you like it or not, Leonie.' His voice was grim and determined. 'You're going to tell me everything this time.'

'There's not a great deal to tell.' Her voice rose above a whisper. 'We were just two mismatched people who didn't realise it until it was too late. Then all the frustrations of it . . . turned it into a nightmare, as much for him as for me. In fact, if I could only have handled the,' her voice cracked, 'the sex side of it better . . .'

'You couldn't have been to blame on your own,' he interrupted.

'But you don't know . . .'

'Right, I don't. But I aim to find out, now.' He rolled off the bed and pulled on a pair of shorts. 'I'll make a cup of coffee. It might be easier to talk in the lounge . . .'

Leonie sighed as he left the room, knowing that he was going to be quite implacable about this. She sat up and reached for her robe.

*   *   *

'. . . I met him at University in Townsville. I was just completing a Bachelor of Arts, majoring in music. He did a series of lectures on Papua New Guinea. They were good—at least I found them interesting . . .'

'What was he? I mean what did he do?'

'He . . . Tom, was an archaeologist. We met socially then after his final lecture. He . . . said he was on six months leave and asked me out to dinner. I went.' She stared at the coffee cup in her hand.

'What was he like?'

She raised her eyes. They were sitting at the dining-room table. 'He was quite a lot older than me and quite different to anyone I'd ever gone out with. He didn't seem to expect any . . . physical contact, which suited me . . .'

'Why?' Guy Richardson asked.

She hesitated. Then she said directly. 'There comes a time when you get tired of being expected to go to bed with someone simply because you're seeing them. Then, when his six months was up, he asked me to marry him.'

'So you married a man you hadn't even kissed?' he said softly and incredulously.

Leonie flushed. 'We had . . . by then. I was—I found it was pleasant and I sometimes found myself thinking of going to bed with him and looking forward to it. But,' she sighed, 'you're right in a way. It was other things that attracted me. Looking back now, I can see that. He was good company, mentally stimulating, he was good-looking . . . I liked the scholarly side of him and I liked the thought of exploring the world and so on. But particularly,' her voice dropped, 'I liked the fact that it all seemed so sane and rational and bore no resemblance to the turbulent kind of relationship my parents had had—hating each other at times as passionately as they had loved, a terrible seesaw until the final break came and then, my mother left in a permanent state of bitterness.'

'How long did it take you work that out? That . . . Tom's attraction for you was mainly that? The dispassionate antithesis of what your parents had?'

'I don't know. It came slowly,' she whispered.

'Go on.'

She said with an effort, 'Things began to go wrong almost from the first night of our honeymoon. I . . . *was* a virgin then and I had no idea how impatient he was, how he'd been holding himself back all those months. It—was a fiasco and it was all my fault . . .'

'Oh, Leonie,' Guy said gently.

'No, I should have understood. But there were so many things I didn't understand about Tom . . . for example, that the fact I didn't get any pleasure from it was like an insult to him, an insult to his manhood. But then that took me some time to work that out, too. I kept thinking it would come right but when it didn't . . . it wasn't that I hated it, just that . . .' She stopped and groped for words.

'He didn't fulfil you?'

'No . . . And because he didn't, he began to be more and more *forceful* and then I did start to hate it.' She took a deep breath. 'That's when I began to . . . pretend,' she said blindly.

'And that did the trick?' Guy asked after a long time.

'It did for him. It didn't do much good for me though. I felt . . . such a fraud. And I'd look at him sometimes and wonder how he could be taken

in. It ... it was like a nightmare. He hated to talk
about it ... it was strange, we could talk about
anything else under the sun but when I tried the
thing that was most important ...' She shrugged.
'Of course, I've telescoped it all. It didn't all
happen in a matter of weeks. We went to live in
Port Moresby and went on expeditions, digs, and
so on. It wasn't all misery but it was there all the
time. I couldn't believe I'd got myself into a
situation like that. And eventually it began to
colour every aspect of our life. I was always tense
and on edge. And he, well there was something
else about him I'd never realised. He was
unbelievably possessive. He resented me having anything to do with practically anyone else. I wanted
to join a little musical group but he wouldn't let
me ... If I went out to do some shopping and
came home later than he thought I should have,
he'd demand to know where I'd been, who I'd
been with.'

'He sounds to me,' Guy said slowly, 'like a
deeply insecure man.'

'I think he was,' Leonie said unhappily.
'Insecure and shy, and from some of the things he
said, I think he basically distrusted women ... I
don't know.'

'Did you think of leaving him?'

'Yes. Often. Particularly as a more and more
chauvinistic side of him began to develop ... he
began to be always putting me down over
anything I said or did ... But I felt *guilty*, too. I
felt that it was all my fault as much as his. I still do
... Then, after we'd been married for about fifteen
months he went on an expedition on his own
and—I don't know if you have ever been flying in
Papua New Guinea but it's hair-raising the way

they fly along ravines and land on little strips that just cling to the mountainside—well, the plane crashed. There were no survivors . . .'

The silence stretched until Guy said finally, 'And you were left with an even bigger load of guilt?'

Leonie stirred restlessly, 'Yes,' she whispered. 'Only some days it wasn't only guilt. It was a . . . boiling sense of resentment, too. Why couldn't he ever talk about it? He wasn't a fool, he wasn't uneducated. And why—I think this torments me more than anything—didn't I see what kind of a man he really was?'

She stared at Guy Richardson until he said, 'My dear, I think we all have secrets we hide from ourselves as well as others. Who knows what his were? And you've admitted some of yours, why you married him. Perhaps he had something in his background as you had, that accounted for it. Have you . . . considered, by the way, that what you planned to do to me, was not only revenge for Anne, but your own revenge against men? For what you suffered firstly because of your father, then your husband?'

Leonie closed her eyes. 'Yes,' she whispered. 'I made a vow . . . after Tom died. That I'd never put myself in a position of such vulnerability again.' She opened her eyes and looked at him very directly. 'I don't think men realise how vulnerable you are, you *feel*, how helpless sometimes. And I swore I'd never let that happen to me again.'

'Yet you did it, Leonie,' he said drily. 'With me.'

'No. That was different. I knew exactly what I was going to do, and *why*.'

'Then found you couldn't ... Did you not stop once to wonder why?'

'Oh yes,' she said bleakly. 'The reason I thought I'd be able to go through with it in the first place was ... well, I thought I've pretended so many times before, I can fake anything now ...' She stopped as his hand clenched whitely, and looked away.

'And then you found out you weren't faking at all. Is that it?'

She stood up and walked over to the window.

'Leonie,' he said grimly.

She turned. 'All right, *yes*. But if you think that makes me happy, it doesn't. All it does is take me back to square one ... where some man is back in power again.' Her eyes glittered with tears and her face was pale and tense. 'I know—I know what you're going to say. That one shouldn't generalise about men or women or anything and normally I'd agree. But this seems to be one thing I can't make myself rationalise. I'm *sorry* ...'

They stared at each other, and his face was pale, too, and set and she swallowed and took a step backwards in sudden fright ...

'*Hell*,' he said then beneath his breath. 'What do you think I'm going to do to you? Beat you up?'

'I ... no,' she said shakily and not very convincingly.

He put a hand to his head and rubbed his brow. 'All right,' he said abruptly, 'we'll forget it all. I'll take you home first thing in the morning.'

She stared at him, speechless and with her lips parted until he smiled queerly and said, 'Isn't that what you want now?'

'I ... yes ...'

'Then don't look so surprised. In fact why don't

you go to bed—you're quite safe—because there's not a lot left of the night and we might as well make the best of it. Good night, my dear.' He stood up and came over to her. 'I'm sorry, too,' he said very quietly.

Then he was gone and she was left staring foolishly after him, feeling curiously . . . bereft?

CHAPTER SEVEN

'Is this it?' Guy said the next morning.

'Yes.' Leonie answered and muttered something beneath her breath as the silver Rolls Royce whispered to a halt in front of the old house. Because not only Spider but also Mr Hallsy were in the front garden, apparently trying to pull down a dead pawpaw tree. And they both looked up with varying expressions of surprise. 'You didn't have to bring me. I could have caught a bus.'

He looked amused. In fact, Leonie thought crossly, he'd looked frequently amused since they'd got up and had breakfast together—amused at her efforts to appear normal, sardonically amused when she'd tried to make a little speech of apology in the car and now, the same thing when she was embarrassed and desperately trying to think of a way to say goodbye . . .

'Well, my dear,' he said as if reading her thoughts. 'This is *au revoir*, I guess. Although I should imagine we'll meet again.'

She looked up swiftly.

'I'm sure I'll be coming to the school musical,' he murmured. 'I've never managed to miss one yet.'

'Oh . . .' She stared into his dark blue eyes with a frown in her own, 'Guy . . .' She stopped and bit her lip in frustration. 'I don't know what to say. You've been . . . very understanding. I appreciate it. I also feel an incredible fool . . .' The words rushed out. 'No doubt you'll feel very relieved to be rid of the Powell sisters by now,' she said with a bitterly wry smile.

'Leonie ...' he started to say something then appeared to change his mind. 'Take care of yourself,' he murmured instead and covered one of her hands with his to just press it gently. 'Here,' he added, 'I'll pass your bag out to you ...'

Fifteen minutes later, Leonie was in her flat, having parried her co-tenants' interested enquiries as best she could. And for a long time, she stood just inside the doorway staring straight ahead, then she dropped her face into her hands and began to cry.

Why? she wondered dimly as the racking sobs refused to be denied. What's wrong with me? I got out of it better than I deserved to ... Why do I feel like this ...?

More to the point, she asked herself when she'd finally achieved some self-control and washed her face and made herself a cup of tea, what exactly is it that I feel? Let down somehow ... as if I can't quite believe he's gone out of my life ... lost ... Yes, all those things and something else, so *small* and as if I've let myself down ...

She stared out of her kitchen window unseeingly for a long time. 'So what does it all mean?' she whispered finally. 'That I'm sorry he didn't keep fighting ... that he gave up on me? Is that it? In your heart of hearts, Leonie, despite your brave, defiant ... foolish sentiments, did you fall just a little in love with Guy Richardson? I think you must have ... It wouldn't be hard to do. The thing is, how different is it from what you felt for Tom?'

She sighed suddenly, because looking back now, it was hard to pin down what she'd first felt for Tom Barton without letting subsequent events

cloud it. Although, one thing was for certain, her
body had never responded to him the way it did to
Guy. But that might be a question of technique,
she mused. Something Tom lacked which Guy
certainly doesn't. Yet because somebody makes
loves well—just that by itself—is it enough to
make you fall *in* love with him?

'Oh hell,' she murmured. 'All I know is that last
night I was so sure of everything and then in a
matter of minutes, I felt as if I'd had the ground
cut away from beneath my feet and now I'm sure
of nothing—except, that I've got the horrible
feeling I'm going to *miss* Guy Richardson. But if
that's the case you'd better get it out of your
system fast, Leonie, because it's a lost cause now
and you made it so all by yourself!'

But the fact that she still had three weeks of school
holiday didn't help. Indeed, it did the opposite in
the sense that it also made her realise what a sort
of guiding force in her life her misplaced desire for
revenge against Claire's father had become. It had
in fact nurtured her through what was a pretty dull
existence. And the realisation of this left her liking
herself even less. It also caused her to reflect that
in the two years since she'd been a widow, she'd
achieved nothing. After packing up and leaving
Port Morseby—there hadn't been a lot to pack up,
she and Tom had lived in a rented, furnished
house—she'd gone back to Townsville and got a
job in an office temporarily until she decided what
to do with her life. She'd inherited some money
from Tom but not a lot and had felt guilty about it
anyway, so she'd donated it to the university's
archeological unit, together with his books and
papers and collection of artefacts. In return, the

unit had gratefully advised her that their annual
prize for best student would be named the Tom
Barton award and she'd felt a little more at peace
for a while, as if she'd done something worthwhile
for Tom. But all the old doubts were still there she
discovered, not to be scotched by a gesture. Her
feeling of inadequacy, that there must have been
something she could have done to prevent her
marriage deteriorating so badly in such a short
time, her feeling that it was an unfinished episode
in her life, and the odd times when she wondered
whether she'd subconsciously wished some disaster
to befall him because, she found, when someone
you're busy disliking, sometimes hating, dies—you
can't help wondering that.

So she'd stayed in Townsville and the months
had gone by and she'd put off even going to see
her sister Anne in Sydney because it was as if she
was in a trough of guilt and recrimination and
bewilderment, and dogged by a sense of failure
that she couldn't pull herself out of. Although the
scarcity of Anne's letters and the tone of them had
worried her, too . . .

But one day the longing to get back into music
had surfaced acutely and she'd begun to look
through the papers for a teaching job and soon
realised she'd have more chance down south. So
she'd moved to Brisbane and applied for several
posts and finally got the one at St Bede's. But
she'd had two months to fill in before starting, and
that was when she'd decided to take a holiday on
Moreton Island—and in a sense, curiously, taken
the first step towards Guy Richardson . . .

She'd been entranced with the island, with its
beauty and also the archeological digs and the
Aboriginal middens being unearthed—nearly two

years spent in Tom's company had left her quite
knowledgeable for an amateur. Also concerned for
the future of Moreton Island, which was why she'd
written the article although she'd had little hope of
getting it published. But it had been like a revival
for her, a sort of spiritual coming-to-life again and
she'd posted it off and finally decided to go to
Sydney to see Anne . . .

The rest is history now, she mused, one day
about a week after Guy Richardson had dropped
her back home. It was a short-lived spiritual
revival, wasn't it?

She was sitting in a grassy stretch of parkland
opposite the Broadwater watching some little
children absorbed in digging in the sand with
bright plastic buckets and spades along the water's
edge. And as she watched she was conscious of
never feeling more lonely in her life, and there'd
been times, with Tom, when his very proximity
had made her feel incredibly lonely because they'd
been such alien personalities then—two people
who lived together and slept with each other but
with their thoughts cut off from each other.

She closed her eyes and lay back on the rug
she'd brought, hoping to doze off in the dappled
sunlight because she wasn't sleeping well at night,
but instead she found herself thinking of Guy
Richardson yet again, of the week they'd spent
together—all the things about him that tormented
her so now. His hands, that were long and strong
but could touch so gently, the feeling of being in
his arms, how he'd only once used his considerable
strength against her and then only briefly . . . one
perfect evening together when they'd eaten Nassi
Goreng and watched *Oliver*. But who's to say, she
argued with herself, that in a closer relationship,

those things wouldn't change? In other words, that my judgment about men has drastically improved—who is to say that? Just considering the matter academically which is all I can do now, anyway, I don't have much evidence of it. The opposite if anything. I seriously misjudged Guy in the first place although I had cause to ... But he's obviously not the kind of man Anne described. For that matter he's not the type of man Tom was, but how do I know he doesn't have his own set of ... foibles? *Then*, there's the big question of myself ...

She sighed and then sat up suddenly and said through her teeth, '*Stop* it, Leonie. Stop thinking about Guy, about Tom, about what's past. Concentrate on the future now ... *Do* it!'

'You all right?' a piping voice said close to her left ear. 'When my Mum talks to herself she reckons she's going mad. Boy, does she get mad sometimes, too!'

Leonie jumped and turned to find her face level with a very blue pair of eyes set in a grubby little face atop a small sturdy person clad in a pair of blue bathers only. A little boy of about five, she judged.

'Oh. Well, it is supposed to be a sign of madness,' she said with a grin. 'You might be right,' she added ruefully. 'Although I'm sure your Mum isn't mad—only me ... Does she know where you are, by the way?'

The boy turned to point to a harrassed looking woman a fair way away who was looking around her distractedly.

'Yes, well,' Leonie said and stood up to gather her things, 'time to get back to her, I reckon. Because she might just be getting mad—in the

cross sense of the word, my little friend. Come
along.'

But the funny thing was how one small boy
catching her talking to herself, affected her—
seemed to snap her out of herself and her morbid,
confused thoughts. And the very next day, she
caught a bus up to Brisbane and spent a week at a
modest motel and doing the things one missed on
the Coast. She went to the new Art Gallery, to a
couple of concerts in the City Hall, to the theatre,
and did some shopping for clothes. Apart from the
gear she'd bought for her trip on the *Marie-Claire*,
she hadn't bought many new clothes for ages and
with winter coming up, it suddenly seemed like a
good idea. She also found herself thinking more
and more of the school musical coming up in two
months time and began to make notes about the
scenery and costumes and looked around for
ideas. Miss Lucas had made it abundantly clear
that while she didn't mind training voices and
choirs, other aspects of the *Pirates of Penzance*
with an all-girl cast could be all Leonie's
department if she so wished it.

'And by golly!' Leonie murmured to herself one
day during that week in Brisbane, 'if I'm going to
do it, why not do it well?'

School started again and even Claire Richardson
only mildly managed to dent Leonie's new-found
composure.

'How was France?'

Claire sighed. 'It was lovely! Although I missed
my father but I met all my French relations this
time—there are dozens of them. For one thing my
mother had two brothers and three sisters.'

'She must have missed her family, your mother.'

'I guess she would have. She only came out to Australia for six months originally—the airline she worked for opened an office in Brisbane and she was sent out to help get it going. Then she met Daddy ... I think that's what I'd like to do—work for an airline. Don't you think it would be a very glamorous job, Miss Powell? Even if you weren't an air hostess and she wasn't, she was in the administrative side but even so, I think it would be terrific!'

'I think it would, too,' Leonie said gently. 'But we do have this music exam coming up in the meantime ...'

The weeks slid by and the chill of autumn crept into the air but Leonie was busy and, she thought, relatively happy.

It took a 'phone-call she received in the staff-room one lunch time to prove to her how relative her state of happiness was.

'Leonie? Is that you? It's Peggy. Sorry to ring you at school but you're not on the 'phone at home, are you?'

'No, I'm not. How are you, Peggy?'

'Fine, dear. Look, Bob and I are giving a party this coming Saturday evening and we'd love you to come along. It's nothing formal, just a get together with some music for those who'd like to dance, a buffet supper ... How does that sound to you? Both Bob and I rather hate the thought of losing contact with you. And,' Peggy hesitated minutely, 'even if you and Guy have ... drifted apart, we feel that's no reason for *us* to drift apart.'

Leonie took a breath. 'Peggy, I appreciate that, I really do but, well, you of all people must understand that ... things are rather awkward between Guy and myself.' She looked around a little warily but no one seemed to be in earshot.

Peggy said, 'My dear, for one thing, I'm not even sure if Guy will be here—he's got some business in Sydney and doesn't quite know when he'll be back but even if he is, I have complete faith in Guy being quite civilised about it, you know.'

Leonie was silent for a moment. Then she said with difficulty, 'I'd really rather not, Peggy. Please don't think I'm being churlish—I, too, would love to keep in contact with you and Bob, but . . .'

'Then no buts!' Peggy said determinedly. 'Forget about what's flowed under the bridge. Life's too short to run scared about things that are in the past. We'll expect you at eight. *So* looking forward to seeing you again, Leonie!' And the 'phone went dead in Leonie's hand. She stared at it helplessly then put it down.

Peggy's 'phone-call came on a Wednesday. Thursday, Friday and Saturday proved to be less than comfortable days for Leonie. One half of her wanted the companionship of people—people she had liked, and particularly Peggy who had tried to do her level best for Anne. But the other half of her, she discovered, was wildly cynical and for a reason Peggy might not guess. Because while Guy might be very civilised about meeting her again, she herself had the horrible feeling that running into Guy Richardson was the last thing she should do to herself.

I've got over it, she thought—whatever it was.

And later, she thought, then if you've got over it, why worry about running into him?

And much later, she thought, why should I cut myself off from the only real social contacts I've

had for years because of him? On the other hand—
what if I haven't really got over it . . .?

I won't go, she told herself on Saturday
morning. But she washed her hair and later, she
ironed one of her new autumn dresses. It was a
honey of a dress, sophisticated yet demure with a
high neckline and long full sleeves in a grey silky
polyester with little flecks of jade green through it.
And because she'd inherited a pair of turquoise
earrings from her mother, she thought as she
ironed, I could put my hair up to show off the
earrings . . .

Which was what she did in the end, but she was
plagued by second thoughts right up until she
stood outside the door of Peggy and Bob's unit.
Then it was too late as another couple emerged
from the lift, guests too, and they all went in
together.

There was no doubting the sincerity of Peggy's
greeting or Bob's and Leonie couldn't help feeling
warmed and glad she'd come. Also, there was no
sign of Guy . . .

Laurel was there, looking outrageous in an
electric-blue satiny boilersuit but like Guy, Brad
was conspicuous by his absence.

'Leonie!' Laurel danced up to her and grabbed
her hand. 'Oh, my, you look perfectly elegant!'

'Thank you, Laurel,' Leonie replied with a grin.
'You look . . . stunning.'

'That's my motto—knock 'em cold! I'm really
pleased to see you, though. I was beginning to
worry that we might never meet again. Now,'
she held up a scarlet-tipped hand, 'you don't
have to make any explanations because while
Guy Richardson is a friend, it makes not the

slightest difference to me if you've fallen out
with him.'

'It . . . I . . .'

'Say no more, pet,' Laurel murmured and put a
hand on her arm. 'Who would you like to meet?'

Several hours later, Leonie wandered on to the
narrow veranda high up above Surfer's and
welcomed the chill of the night air. Her skin was
damp with perspiration because the party had
become very lively indeed and she'd danced as
much as anyone and as the time passed and it
became more and more unlikely that Guy would
not attend, she'd relaxed more and more.

There was an interesting selection of guests that
she'd enjoyed meeting and talking to and they all
seemed to be the kind of people who were warmly
friendly.

I didn't realise how much I've missed just
normal social company, she reflected as she leant
back against the wall and closed her eyes. But I've
really led an incredibly solitary life . . . well, ever
since I married Tom. He didn't seem to need
company, besides being ridiculously jealous if I so
much as looked sideways at another man . . .

She sighed and opened her eyes and turned to
go in and stopped dead. Because across the room
she could see a tall figure in a dark suit, a late
arrival by the look of it. Guy . . .

Her heart started to hammer and her mouth
went dry and she wished desperately that she could
suddenly become invisible. But he lifted his head
and looked straight at her and his eyes narrowed
immediately in recognition.

And all she was able to do in return was stare at
him helplessly, and know with a sickening lurch of

her heart, that just the sight of Guy Richardson did the strangest things to her—made her knees feel weak so that she wanted to clutch the doorway for support, made her oddly breathless and filled her at the same time with a sense of despair and disbelief that this could be happening to her . . .

It was she who looked away first but because someone was talking to her, a man she'd danced with before.

'I'm sorry . . .'

He had thick spectacles and she'd forgotten his name but not his rather shy smile.

'I only said if you could put up with me standing on your toes again, would you like to dance?'

'I . . . thank you. I'm sorry but I've forgotten your name. I've met so many people tonight it's . . .' She heard herself talking light-headedly, rambling on and when he told her his name, she forgot it almost immediately. But to be dancing with someone, to be active, helped and there was someone else to take his place for the next dance.

Peggy and Bob had imported a miniature dance floor to put over the carpet at one end of their large living-room and it had become more and more crowded and as soon as one record finished, some obliging soul would pop their favourite kind of dance music on to the hi-fi set with the result that from waltzing you could find yourself bopping, then disco dancing or trying to do the tango—with much hilarity.

But as the music clicked off this time someone dimmed the lights and some soft, slow music started and Guy Richardson loomed up in front of her.

'Leonie.' He inclined his head briefly.

'H-hello,' she stammered. 'I didn't think you were coming—I mean, well, it must be very late,' she said lamely.

'I didn't expect you to be here. Shall we dance? We're only getting in the way otherwise.'

'I . . . all right.'

They danced in silence, Leonie mechanically and with her whole body tense because she was afraid, deathly afraid of this close contact with him and what it would do to her, how it would give her away. And afraid, too, because the few words he'd spoken to her had been abrupt and she'd caught a hard glint in his dark blue eyes as they'd rested on her flushed face, and seen his mouth set at her faltering greeting.

But perhaps what frightened her most was the fact that even if he was angry, it didn't alter the effect he was having on her, the way his hand on the small of her back seemed to be burning through the thin stuff of her dress, the way his body moved which recalled to mind much more intimate memories of it, so that a slow heat began to burn again in her cheeks and all her nerve-ends seemed to be pitched too finely, quiveringly like tautened strings until it became an incredible effort to move her feet in time to the music . . .

But finally the track ended and she took a breath as everyone stopped dancing expectantly, and said huskily, 'I'm sorry, but I think I've had enough. I . . . actually, I was thinking of going home a while ago.'

He looked down at her and she shivered suddenly at the mockery she saw in his eyes and she looked downwards hurriedly because she couldn't bear to see it although she knew she deserved it. Why . . . oh, why did I *come*! She wondered miserably and started to turn away but he put a hand on her arm and one under her chin to tilt her head up.

'Still doing that, Leonie?' he said barely audibly but with so much contempt, she died a little inside. 'Still hiding from people,' he went on. 'Not to mention yourself.'

'I . . . no . . . I don't know what you mean,' she whispered.

'Then dance with me this one last time and I'll tell you,' he drawled and in one way she was glad the music had started again and that someone had dimmed the lights even more although it meant the torture of another dance with him, because otherwise she was sure she would do something incredibly foolish like bursting into tears. But as he drew her back into his arms, she stiffened again.

'Don't,' he murmured. 'I'm not going to *do* anything to you. Relax, dance, like this . . . it's easy. See?' His eyes taunted her as he swung her round to the music, his lead so sure, so rhythmic, she had to follow. 'And again . . .' He led her expertly through the slow foxtrot. 'There,' he said, his lips twisted derisively. 'Is that so hard on you?'

'Guy . . .' Her mouth trembled and a shimmer of tears came to her eyes.

'Leonie?' He raised his eyebrows sardonically when she found it impossible to go on and she bit her lip and stumbled but that only made him tighten his hold on her and force her to concentrate on the steps again.

I can't stand much more of this, she thought wildly, even if I deserve it . . .

'Why did you come?' he said then.

But she knew that to speak would break the last

slender thread of control she had, and she shook her head wordlessly and looked blindly over his shoulder.

'Not to see me, I gather.' His words were clipped.

She still couldn't speak.

'But according to Peggy, you knew I might be here. Isn't that so, Leonie?' he said compellingly.

'Yes,' she whispered.

'Look at me . . .'

She did, finally.

'So why?' The words were softly spoken but there was no mistaking the intent behind them. And she shivered again because she knew he wasn't going to allow her to escape without answering.

She licked her lips. 'I . . . to see Peggy and Bob. I *liked* them.'

'Is that all?' His probing dark blue gaze was merciless.

A shudder seemed to rack her body. 'I . . .'

'Say it, Leonie. Otherwise I'll say it for you.'

She closed her eyes and didn't doubt that in this mood, he would, and that he'd be right. 'I . . . to see you,' she whispered, and knew it to be true. In fact, she realised she'd known it from the moment she'd looked across the crowded room and seen him, known it painfully in her heart of hearts and known, too, that she'd only been kidding herself when she'd thought she'd been glad he wasn't there . . .

'And why did you want to see me?' he queried with something she couldn't name glinting in his eyes.

'Because . . .' What was in her eyes, the anguish, was plain to be interpreted, but as she spoke, she straightened her shoulders in an unconsciously gallant little gesture as of someone prepared to bear the consequences of their own folly. 'Because, ever since we parted,' her voice cracked, 'I haven't been able to stop thinking about you. And even when I thought I wasn't, I . . . it was like a weight pressing down on me. Which, after what I said to you that night, the way I acted, is incredible to me—but even more so to you, I should imagine,' she finished, her low words tinged with bitter self-mockery.

They'd stopped dancing properly as she spoke and were only marking time to the music and he didn't say anything for about a minute, just searched her face sombrely. Then something like a sigh seemed to escape him and he brought up one hand to cup the back of her head and press it into his shoulder.

'I think we need to get out of here,' he said finally. 'I think we need to be able to *talk* in private.' His hand slid down and around and he lifted her chin so that he could see into her eyes. 'Will you come with me?'

She stared at him through a mist of tears, then she moved her head in a silent, despairing gesture of assent.

He accomplished it with a minimum of fuss. All the same, Leonie caught Bob's glance of curiosity, Peggy's one of restrained concern, and from across the room, Laurel narrowed her eyes then waved her fingers.

But she felt too weary and inexpressibly drained to care about the speculation they were causing and once in the lift, she stood obediently beside Guy with her hand in his and allowed herself to be born upwards . . .

Then the door of his unit was closed behind them, the world closed out, and it looked exactly the same to her—as if she'd never left as she stood in the middle of the living-room, looking around, her face white and strained as he switched on a couple of lamps and walked towards her and took her in his arms . . .

'Guy . . .' His name got choked in her throat.

'Not yet,' he murmured and began to kiss her hair, her eyelids. 'Is this what you thought about? And this?' His wandering lips sought the soft slender line of her throat. 'I have been, too. Don't cry,' he said softly as the tears slid down her cheeks and he kissed them lingeringly.

'I feel such a fool . . .'

'Why? It's no crime to change your mind.'

'I . . . I don't know if I have about everything . . .'

'Leonie,' he said against the corner of her mouth, 'kiss me . . .'

'Oh, Guy,' she wept, 'I can't *think* . . .'

But those were the last words she said for a long time. His lips were impossible to resist and the feel of his strong, hard body moulding hers, enveloping her so that she felt like a slender wand, made especially to bend to his will, overcame her puny defences totally.

Until at last, he lifted his head and she swayed in his arms and he picked her up and sat down on the settee with her in his lap.

'How . . . how would it be,' he said in a curiously husky voice and one hand fiddling with some wayward strands of her hair that had come down, 'if . . . we made a pact to have a completely open kind of relationship? No strings, no vows, no constraints, no moving in with each other ... Just to be taken one day at a time, at *your* pace.'

She lay with her head pillowed against his arm, her eyes huge and dark in the pallor of her face, her dishevelled hair framing it with a kind of sensuous abandon. And her breathing was unsteady so that her breasts rose and fell visibly and a tiny pulse beat erratically at the base of her throat. She lifted a hand and touched her lips which felt swollen and bruised then, in an involuntary gesture, touched those fingers to his mouth.

He caught her hand and kissed the palm then folded it into his.

'Do you really mean that? But ... it's unfair, to you.'

He smiled slightly. 'Beggars can't be choosers ...'

'Guy ...'

'Well actually, that aside,' his lips quirked, 'it's the sensible way to go about it really. Isn't it? I mean when two people find themselves wanting each other—and I think *that's* been established.' He lifted her hand to his mouth and kissed her fingers again gently. 'It's still wise not to rush into anything ... binding. And we're not children, Leonie. We've both been through this before in one way or another. I think we're entitled to ... look upon ourselves as mature enough to handle it.'

Her hand moved in his. 'What if ... what if one of us wants to end it and the other doesn't?'

'Then I think that's where we might have an advantage. We should be—that's what I meant about being mature—we should be able to face a lost cause. You can't totally love someone who doesn't love you in return. Pride may dictate to you that they *should* reciprocate but pride and ego, for example, may be what Tom suffered from. Brought about by a crippling sense of insecurity . . .'

Leonie took a breath. 'Do you think he knew that I didn't love him?'

'Perhaps. Only to blame yourself for that *is* foolish, Leonie. Love,' something in his voice changed, 'comes where it comes. It can't be manufactured.'

'The thing is,' she said very quietly, 'how to know it. That's a mistake I did make—and he had to pay for.'

'You both paid for it. But that's a mistake many, many people make, you were not unique, believe me. But to . . . feel you have to go on paying for it, Leonie, is only compounding it.'

'But,' her voice quivered, 'can you understand why I . . .'

'Oh yes. It's left you hurt and very wary. That's natural. In fact, the more sensitive you are, the more you feel these things. But to live the rest of your life branding yourself as a *failure* . . .'

He stopped as her lashes lifted suddenly and she stared up at him unhappily as the thought ran through her mind that somehow, Guy Richardson could read her innermost thoughts . . .

'So it's true.' His lips barely moved.

'I . . .'

'I wish I could tell you how untrue that is. But mere words won't do it . . . There's one special way that would though. If only you'd let me.'

She turned her face into his shoulder.

'I told you the conditions. I'll stick to them, I swear.' He stroked her hair.

She was silent for a long time. Then she took a long quivering breath and turned her face to him. 'A—all right.'

'Talking is what helps at times like this,' he said later. 'If you don't like what I'm doing, tell me.'

'I ... I like very much what you're doing,' she said breathlessly.

'Good. But you're still tense ...'

'I can't seem to help it.'

'Then I'm doing something wrong.'

'No ...' she said uncertainly as his hand moved slowly down from her erect nipples round the curve of her hip to her thighs to slide between them. 'How ... how can you be so patient?' she asked with a catch in her voice.

His teeth flashed in the lamplight, in a sudden grin. 'It's my middle name, Guy Patience Richardson ...'

She turned her head on the pillow and couldn't help smiling back. Then she caught her breath at what his wandering hand was doing to her, very gently but all the same ...

'What is it?' he said with a frown in his eyes. 'Am I hurting you?'

'No ...' she said hastily then bit her lip. 'Only, sometimes it's ... it's almost unbearable. Not because it hurts but ... I just don't know how to explain it.'

His hand left her body and he pulled her into his arms and she relaxed perceptibly.

'Do you know,' she said shyly after a while, 'what I like most? It probably sounds crazy to you, but this. To be held close ...'

'Why should it be crazy?' he said softly. 'I like it, too.'

'It ... well it doesn't seem very adventurous ...'

'If we like it, who cares? Anyway, it seems to be having a very adventurous effect on me in case you hadn't noticed ... I might have to change my name. Leonie,' his voice was muffled against her throat, 'you're so very lovely and so good to hold like this.' He moved his hand up and down her back and she shivered with pleasure, at the feel of his skin against hers, the hard planes of his body against the soft, slightness of her own, and she began to stroke his back in return.

And after a time it was as if all her nervous tension had drained away, and she felt boneless and cherished and warm and as if her body was opening up to his joyfully. And not even the slight pain she felt because it had been some time, dimmed her need to welcome him into her, to give herself to him as generously as she could.

But what all but took the breath away was the sensation that began to wash through her, wave upon wave of feeling although his body was moving quite gently on hers ...

Something she'd never experienced before and she cried out softly in wonder and surprise and clung to him, unable to believe that it was finally happening to her, and that it had come about so simply yet at the same time it was the most moving thing that had ever happened to her. Indescribable, breath-taking, giving her a sense of completeness she'd guessed she'd lacked but never known how much ...

Then she was saying his name over and over again and holding him, ready to die for him and willing him to experience this miracle, too, because for it to be a mutual thing would set the seal of supremity on it, she knew.

They lay quite still, side by side for a long time afterwards, holding hands, getting their breath back.

Then he turned to her and took her back into his arms and kissed her. 'See,' he murmured, 'you did it. Wonderfully . . .'

'Oh, Guy,' she whispered, '*you* did it.' She touched his face with trembling fingers. 'How can I ever thank you?'

He kissed her fingers. 'One way—by accepting that it wasn't so much my doing but the fact that you trusted me enough to tell me what you liked, what you wanted. That's what did it.'

'All the same, if you hadn't had the patience . . .'

He was quiet for a time. Then he said, 'Will you spend the day with me?'

'I . . . provided you don't want to go out and about,' she said with a sudden smile curving her lips.

He touched her mouth. 'That wasn't what I had in mind.'

'Good. Because I've only got my best dress . . .'

'Oh . . . Actually, what I thought of doing mostly, doesn't require a lot of clothes. The less the better in fact. And for . . . in between times, meals—I guess we should eat—you could wear something of mine . . .'

'Heavens,' she said faintly, 'what have I let myself in for?'

'Well,' he said, 'perhaps I should have mentioned this earlier but while I may be a patient man, I've also been a . . . starving man in one sense of the word for a little while now. Starved of you . . .' He stroked her hair but there was a glint of laughter in his eyes.

'You make me sound like a feast.' She tried to sound indignant but didn't quite achieve it.

'Mmm. A beautiful one though . . .'

'Oh well,' she capitulated, 'if you keep paying me compliments, I guess I could stand it. Guy . . .' She sobered suddenly and stared deep into his eyes.

'What is it?' he asked finally.

'It's nothing. Nothing. Just . . . thank you.' And she buried her head in his shoulder and after a while, fell asleep in his arms.

They slept late. Then she made them some brunch and they watched an old black-and-white movie on television, lying together on the floor of the den and talking through it. He told her a bit about Claire's mother and the tragic illness that had cut her young life short.

'It just didn't make sense. I couldn't accept that it had to happen, not for a long time. Then, although I can never forget completely, I found that time dims your pain and I realised I was accepting it and making a new life and that was hard too . . . you feel as if you're being unfaithful. Thank God I had Claire. For a long time she was the only thing that gave my life any purpose. And now, it would be true to say, she's the light of my life. What do you think of her? She's the living image of her mother . . .'

Leonie smiled gently. 'She's a darling,' she said sincerely. 'I . . .' She stopped, realising she'd been going to say that she'd love to see him and Claire together, but she thought better of it. 'Oh,' she said instead to his look of enquiry, 'I'm not the only one who thinks so, either. Even Miss Lucas can't resist Claire.'

'She's pretty taken with you, too, you know. She said to me once . . . well,' he grinned suddenly, 'I might tell you that one day.'

'Why not now?'

'Oh, I wouldn't want to see you get a swollen head,' he teased. 'By the way, this movie, which we're not watching has come to a pretty interesting stage, had you noticed?'

'No.'

'Well it has. A stage that's giving me ideas . . .'

Leonie lifted herself on to one elbow. 'Why? What are they doing? Oh . . .'

'Mmm . . . They're about to go to bed.'

'But they've been up a lot longer than we have. I mean . . .'

'I know what you mean. They've been tormenting themselves for months if the few bits of the story I've gleaned are anything to go by.'

'I thought you said you were a patient man . . .'

'*You* said that first.' He pulled her close and slid his hands under his shirt that she was wearing.

'You agreed . . .'

'Are you giving me a hard time, by any chance?' he asked with a glint of laughter in his eyes. 'Is this the reward I get for so much patience?'

'Oh no,' she answered softly and curved her arms around his neck. 'I thought you were never going to ask!'

'You look . . . different.'

Leonie turned on the dressing-table stool. Guy was standing behind her, dressed and with his car keys in his hand. She was dressed, too, in the grey-green dress and she'd been brushing her hair. The sky was darkening outside the windows of the bedroom.

'Better or worse?' she said lightly.

'No . . . you look happy.'

'I am,' she said softly and stood up. 'All thanks to you . . .'

He studied her soberly. Then he said with a touch of wryness, 'I shouldn't ask this, in view of our agreement but when can I see you again?'

'Whenever you'd like to,' she whispered. 'Agreements can be . . . bent a little, can't they?'

'If you say so . . .'

'Yes. Yes . . . I don't really want to go home now but I *should*. For one thing there's school tomorrow and for another, Spider will worry about me. I didn't tell him I wouldn't be home. And . . .' She stopped.

'You don't have to explain, my dear,' he murmured. 'I was the one who said it . . . about rushing into things. That still stands. But thank you,' he tilted her chin up with his fingers, 'for saying you'd like to stay.'

'Guy . . .'

'No . . . Kiss me instead, Leonie.' His eyes glinted a little wickedly. 'It might see me through until—shall we make it Wednesday night? Or after school? I could pick you up at home. What time?'

'Four o'clock . . .'

CHAPTER EIGHT

THE next four weeks went by in a daze for Leonie.

She saw Guy every two or three days and spent three week-ends with him. The other week-end was Claire's monthly week-end off school and by mutual, unspoken agreement, Leonie stayed home and worked furiously to catch up on what she was doing on scenery and costumes for the musical. Spider proved invaluable on the matter of scenery and even Mr Hallsy lent a hand—a very artistic hand at that.

'You must both come,' Leonie said gratefully. 'As my guests.'

But really, every minute of those four weeks was spent thinking of Guy. When she was away from him, she thought of him making love to her, making her respond to him sometimes just simply as it had happened the first time, sometimes more adventurously, as she thought of it. So that the lovely agony was prolonged and her body was racked with desire and her hands and her lips sought him with an abandon she'd not believed she was capable of.

One such time had been a Saturday night on board the *Marie-Claire*. They'd fished and swum although only briefly because the water was colder now, and finally anchored for the night in a spot off Stradbroke known, appropriately she thought with a wry grin, as The Bedrooms.

'Good spot,' he said perfectly seriously.

'Oh, definitely,' she agreed. 'For what you have in mind.'

'What do *you* have in mind?'

'I have in mind . . . what you have in mind,' she said ruefully. 'I can't think why . . .'

He reached for her. 'You're very well dressed in that case,' he said.

'It's cold.' It was true. With the fall of darkness, a damp chill had entered the air and there was a slight mist rising up from the water. She'd donned her jeans and a navy blue jumper although the cabin door was firmly closed against the night, and the silent swell of the water was only felt, not heard.

But later, much later, it wasn't cold. And he said, 'That wasn't such a bad idea after all, was it? How do you feel?'

Leonie stretched luxuriously. They were both lying on the double bed in his cabin and the sheets were rumpled and the mirror panelled wall opposite glimmered faintly in the dim light filtering in from a high, white moon above.

Her breasts were still tender in the aftermath of love and her hair was spread on the pillow in disarray. 'I feel,' she said slowly and reached out a hand to touch him, 'wanton, shameless—a hussy. I don't know what you must think of me.'

He smiled in the darkness, 'If that's an invitation to me to tell you . . .'

'No. Guy,' she half sat up and reached for the sheet, 'I did . . . you make me do things I've never dreamed of doing. I . . . it's strange.' She shivered slightly.

He pulled her back into his arms. 'You were magnificent,' he said huskily. 'Don't regret it. Because it makes me feel fantastic when you're wanton—as you put it.' He kissed her lingeringly.

'And when I'm not,' she whispered after a while.

'It isn't always like that.' She felt her cheeks grow hot at the memory of it.

'It's a matter of mood, too. For example, we could make love now, again, quite differently, but it would be just as good in its own way ... I'll show you.'

He did. But this time, at his direction, she did nothing at all. Just lay still, soothed and caressed by the lightest touch of his hands and his lips, almost drowsy, as if this was another dimension of the world he'd opened up for her. And the climax she achieved was sweet and warm and comforting ...

'The perfect way to end a perfect day,' she murmured sleepily. 'One day I'll do that for you, if you want me to ...'

'I could think of nothing nicer.'

It became apparent over those four weeks, too, that her new state of happiness was there for all to see.

Spider commented on it. 'The man with the Rolls?' he added.

She coloured faintly but nodded.

'Ah, well,' he said with a tinge of wry regret in his voice, 'I should tell you to watch out for yourself, but you're only young once ...'

Claire Richardson was another person who commented on it. 'Are you in love, Miss Powell?' she asked directly during one music lesson.

'What makes you think that?'

They were sitting side by side at the piano.

'You look different,' Claire said honestly. 'And Jane Sutherland,' Jane was a girl Leonie found a little hard to take because she was a fount of immature wisdom, 'said you must have found yourself a man ... Oh!' Claire put a hand to her lips. 'I didn't mean to say it like that. Only ...'

'That's how Jane put it,' Leonie said drily, thinking irritably at the same time, that even if Jane was *right* for once, it needn't be put like that ...

'Well, yes. I'm sorry,' Claire said anxiously. 'But you do look ... different. Lovelier than ever,' she added sincerely.

Leonie flinched inwardly and thought, oh God, if only you knew, Claire.

'By the way, I want to introduce you to my father at the musical, Miss Powell,' Claire went on. 'I've told him about you—that you're quite the nicest, prettiest teacher I've ever had, music or otherwise.'

'You're a flatterer, Claire,' Leonie managed to say.

Claire grinned and suddenly Leonie saw Guy in her so much it all but took her breath away. 'Sometimes,' Claire confessed, 'but not in this case. He said he'd really like to meet you!'

'I ... that would be nice. Do ... you miss not having a mother, Claire?' The words came out involuntarily but Leonie's hands trembled because she knew what depth of her heart had prompted them ...

'Sometimes,' Claire said a little sadly. 'But then I sometimes think, if you haven't got your *own* mother, it might be even harder to have a stepmother. And Daddy and I get along really well on our own, you know. It,' she hesitated, then said with a wisdom beyond her years, 'might be hard to share him with someone now. But of course if he fell in love, I'd make the best of it. And just hope it was someone I liked. But I think my mother was

the one great love of his life. That can happen to
people, can't it, Miss Powell?'

'I ... guess it can ...'

'Only *three* days to go,' a booming voice
interrupted them, approaching down the corridor.
'Three days! We'll never make it! Where is
everyone?'

Claire giggled. 'Miss Lucas,' she whispered.
'Every years she gets into a state about the
musical ...'

As it turned out it was also three days to go before
the blow fell, three days during which she didn't
see Guy because he was away on business. So from
having that rather revealing conversation, revealing
not only on account of Claire's sentiments, but her
own, she was without his reassuring presence ...
Alone with the turbulence of her thoughts ...
Have I fallen in love with him? So deeply that I'd
like to marry him, spend the rest of my life with
him and not care in the slightest that I once swore
to myself I'd never let another man have that kind
of power over me? Why else would I be worrying
about Claire?

'And worrying,' she whispered to herself, 'about
what he really feels for me, and whether Claire was
right ... about the one great love of his life? After
all, if I hadn't gone to Peggy's party ...'

Then on the morning of the musical, she woke
up with a sudden pounding heart and looked at
her diary. But no amount of counting back altered
anything, no mistakes had been made and she
stared blindly before her and considered the
possibility that she was pregnant.

'No,' she said hoarsely. 'Oh no. It was only that
one night, the first time that I didn't have any

protection. It would be a million to one chance, surely? But I'm never late ... and this is over a week now. Why did I *forget*! Not that it would have made any difference but ... oh God!'

The rest of the day was like a nightmare, only worse. It became tinged with a desperate irony. When she got home from school there was a letter from Anne. The first she'd received for months. In fact the whole question of Anne had been something she'd shelved after the shock of discovering how her sister had lied, because she'd not known what she could do.

But it appeared, as she read the letter, that Anne herself was now handling her own salvation.

'This is the hardest letter I've ever had to write,' Leonie read, 'because I have to tell you that I deliberately misled you ...' Her lips moved as she read on and it was all there, in black and white, Peggy and Guy's version of what had really happened to Anne, written in Anne's own hand ... 'You might be wondering what's finally brought me to my senses, Leonie,' she wrote on, 'but I've found out that I'm going to have a baby—we're going to have a baby ...'

Leonie let her hand with the letter in it fall in disbelief, then made herself read on. '... It really made me stop and think. And I thought, I can at least try to sort out my life now. It's the least I can do. Ron is willing to try, too. So that's what we'll be doing and that's why I had to write to you and tell you this in an effort to start all over again with a clean slate. Please write soon ... Your loving, humble but determined sister, Anne.'

Leonie sank into a chair and felt like laughing and crying at the same time. She could only be happy for Anne but the coincidence of it, if she herself was pregnant, seemed incredible to her, especially in the circumstances. But then the whole business has been incredible, hasn't it? she thought. But what am I going to *do*? If I am?

The nature of the day though, gave her no opportunity to do anything constructive. She had less than an hour to get dressed and have a hasty meal before getting back to school. And if the ordeal of the musical wasn't enough by itself even for someone in an untroubled frame of mind, there was the burden of having to meet Guy . . .

'It went well,' Miss Lucas said in hushed tones as the final curtain rang down on the *Pirates of Penzance*. 'Apart from Clarissa forgetting her entrance in the second act and Marcia persistently singing in the wrong key and . . . but thanks to you, my dear, it went well,' she said to Leonie in tones of amazement and gratitude.

'I didn't do much . . .'

'I think you'll find it was the most successful and inspired musical we've put on for many years, Helen dear. See if I'm not wrong! Well, now that's over we have a trauma of another kind to deal with. Refreshments in the refectory with the parents. I always feel like a block of wood when I have to deal with parents. What about you?'

'It's my first time.'

'Hah! You'll learn! Just don't be critical of their little darlings tonight even if they are tone deaf and have a touch like a herd of elephants. But I'll be there to lend moral support!'

She was, too. In fact they were both the object of much interest and many congratulations and had the added honour of the headmistress standing beside them to introduce them . . .

'Yes, I thought it was particularly good, Mr Stevens. Good-evening, Mrs Stevens. And of course it was all due to our Miss Lucas and her new assistant Miss Powell. I don't believe you've met Miss Powell . . .'

Leonie shook hands time and time again then a subtle change in the headmistress's tone took her notice while she was still talking to Marcia-of-the-wrong-key's parents and when she looked up, she saw why. It was Guy dressed in a sober dark suit and a white silk shirt and looking urbane and slightly amused because Miss Lucas was now talking to him and she, too, had adopted a slightly coy manner. At least I'm not alone, she thought with something like despair. He has a devastating effect on most females . . .

'Oh, well a lot of the credit goes to our Miss Powell, Mr Richardson,' Miss Lucas was saying now. 'Plus the fact that she has a way with the girls . . . But you haven't met her yet. Allow me. Helen dear,' she boomed, 'this is Claire Richardson's father—oh, there you are, Claire. Why don't you get your father a cup of coffee and a sandwich?'

'How do you do, Miss Powell?' Guy said and stretched out his hand.

Leonie put hers into it and hesitated infinitesimally before looking up. Claire was telling Miss Lucas her father had already had a cup of coffee with an oddly stubborn note in her voice.

'How do you do, Mr Richardson?' she murmured. Their gazes caught and held and her hand moved restively in his before he let it go.

His eyes narrowed. 'What's wrong?' he said audibly only to her.

'Nothing.' She swallowed and tried to smile. 'Nerves, I guess and reaction. And . . .'

'The fact that this is a bit of a farce? I . .'

'Oh, I understand that,' she interrupted and turned as Claire tugged at her sleeve, her little skirmish with Miss Lucas over and won apparently.

'Well, what do you think of him?' Claire asked enthusiastically, her face alight with pride.

'I . . .'

'Don't answer that, Miss Powell,' Guy said smoothly and with a faint grin. 'Claire, honey, that's not the kind of question you put to people.'

'Why not? I've been dying for you two to meet!'

'I'm very pleased to meet your father, Claire,' Leonie murmured.

'No more than I am to meet you, Miss Powell,' Guy replied but with a glint in his dark blue eyes that brought a faint flush to her cheeks. And that was when Miss Lucas intervened again.

'Well, I don't know about you, Helen, but I'm parched!' she announced.

'Yes, I am a bit, too.'

'Oh, I'll get you a cup of coffee, Miss Powell,' Claire offered brightly. 'You stay and talk to Daddy. I don't know if I can carry two cups, Miss Lucas,' she added ingeniously. 'They tend to spill.'

'I'll come, child,' Miss Lucas said and departed with Claire.

'Claire is a minx at times,' Guy said.

'She's very proud of you.'

'She's also . . . Leonie, there is something wrong,' he said abruptly.

'No . . . Guy . . . it's nothing. I'm just all strung up. This was my first . . . production.'

'Let me take you home. Later of course.'

'No. It would look ... anyway, the school is providing a taxi.'

'I don't care how it looks. Anyway, it's been three days.'

'I don't think I'd be much good to you to-night ...' Her voice cracked slightly.

'If you think the only reason I want to be with you is to sleep with you, you're mistaken,' he said on an oddly grim note.

She looked around in sudden fright but no-one seemed to be listening. All the same, she said nervously, 'Guy, this isn't the time or the place. I ...' She tailed off helplessly.

His mouth hardened. 'Obviously not. What did you think I was going to do tonight? Proclaim to the whole world that we are lovers? Is that why you're in such a state?'

She drew a gasping little breath. '*No*. And I'm not.'

He surveyed her unsmilingly for a moment. Then he said unemotionally, 'You're a bad liar, Leonie. I'll leave it up to you to let me know the *right* time and place. Here comes your coffee. So nice to have met you, Miss Powell,' he raised his voice slightly and turned away.

Claire looked fleetingly disappointed as she handed Leonie a cup and saucer but Miss Lucas appeared again so she drifted off to her father's side.

'Lovely man,' Miss Lucas said, *sotto voce* for her, with a sigh. 'Such a pity he hasn't got a wife. It seems a waste. Mind you, from what one hears on the grapevine he isn't exactly companionless if you know what I mean.' She winked girlishly.

Leonie sipped her coffee and found it almost

choked her. Yes, I know what you mean, she thought. So well . . . But I wonder what you would think, Miss Lucas—for that matter anyone else here tonight—if they knew that I was one of those . . . companions? That the last time I was with Guy Richardson, three days ago, he undressed me very slowly article by article and touched me and caressed me until I was quite mindless with desire. Can you picture that? Your Miss Powell . . .

But now he's walked away from me although it is an impossible situation even leaving aside what he *doesn't* know. Yet he's angry, but what does he expect? It didn't take long to come, our first argument, she thought with a tinge of unhappy bitterness. Oh, God, will this day ever end?

School was disorganised the next day, as was to be expected. But some music lessons went ahead, one of them Claire's. And it was from Claire Leonie learnt that Guy had gone to Darwin on business. It had apparently been an unexpected trip because he'd rung up the school first thing in the morning to let them know in case of emergencies. He would be away, Claire said, for nearly a week. And for the life of her Leonie wasn't sure whether to be happy or sad. It certainly gave her a bit of a breathing space. It also, she found, left her with a quite frightening sense of being alone that was at variance with the spurt of bitterness she'd felt last night.

And it forced her to examine that sudden uprush of hostility, on both sides, that had occurred in the refectory after the musical . . .

He did guess something was wrong, she reflected. If only I could have told him but first I at least need to be sure. And what I said about not

being any good to him, was unfair I guess. Unfair
enough to warrant him getting angry? Perhaps . . .
Oh, damn, I feel as if I'm going around in circles.
But there's one thing I must do. I must make sure.
Tomorrow . . .

'Tomorrow' was a Saturday and when she got
back from the doctor, she shut herself into her flat
and lay down on the bed and tried to think.

A baby . . . my baby, our baby . . . A child,
perhaps a boy who would grow up to look like his
father, a half-brother or sister for Claire although
now only a tiny seed within her. The result of the
most momentous thing that had ever happened to
her . . .

But what does it really mean? she asked herself.

That it closes off all other options to us?

Once he knows, he might think he has to marry
me whether that was his intention or not. Perhaps
it was? But how can I be sure? *He* said it wasn't
wise to rush into anything binding—this would be
like being pitchforked into it . . .

And I can understand why he wouldn't rush
into marriage. For one thing there's Claire, the
light of his life, and for all that he now accepts her
mother's death, does it mean he can love someone
else the way he loved her? Claire doesn't think
so . . .

'But he must have had some plans for us,' she
whispered to herself with tears blurring her vision.
'Only, why should he have, really? I didn't
precisely come across as the kind of person to
make plans around, did I? In fact at one stage, he
obviously wrote me off as a lost cause,' she
grimaced at that oft-recurring phrase, 'someone he
was attracted to but in the end not so desperately

attracted that he couldn't help himself. Oh God, what a mess!'

She cried silently into the pillow for a time, then blew her nose and got up to make herself a cup of tea and sat by the window with it. Spider was mowing the lawn but she didn't even see him.

As for me, she thought finally, as for my intentions, I've had none lately. I've just gone along one day at a time, dazed and helpless, like a child ... Unable to believe what was happening to me, unable to give it a name. Or afraid to? Perhaps.

There is one option open to me, she thought then. I don't have to have this baby.

But the thought brought a cold sweat to her brow and a haunting chill to her heart and she knew in that instant that she could no more deliberately lose this baby than she could fly.

Does that say it all? she asked herself with a suddenly terrified look in her eyes. I think it does. I *want* Guy's baby, even if I'm on my own, even if I lose my job which I will, even if means having to live on a single parent's pension until ... until ... I couldn't want to go through all that unless— unless I loved the father of this baby, could I?

'But what kind of life is that for a child?' she murmured desolately then. 'And what right do I have to make that decision on my own? It is his child, too ... The right to protect myself from what could be ... become another loveless, one-sided marriage? If ... if he'd told Claire about us, I might feel more confident. Then again, it hasn't been very long since we've been ... lovers. Only four weeks or so. Which brings me back to square one—we haven't had *time* to know what it really is for us. Even me ... who's to say the ... sexual side of it hasn't been a real revelation to me. Who's to say it's not *that*? Even if I do want his baby ... It didn't take us long to get angry with each other. But could I have felt so very much with someone I didn't like and admire and respect, and *love*? And could he have ... he seemed to enjoy it too. He's said, all along he's said he *wanted* me. But Tom wanted me, too. Is it necessarily the same thing as love, for a man? Oh, hell, what am I going to do?'

Several days later she was as confused as ever and still basically stunned by it all. And she hadn't heard from Guy and didn't know if he was back—she couldn't seem to find any reasonable way of asking Claire. But she could clearly remember his words—I'll leave it up to you to let me know the right time and place ...

Then things were taken out of her hands in an unexpected way. She got to school one morning only to be violently ill, which left her feeling dizzy and faint.

And it was as if fate could find no better place for this to happen to her than in the headmistress's suite of offices which fortunately had a bathroom attached, the only fortunate thing about the whole incident, she'd thought dimly at first.

She'd been summoned as soon as she'd arrived at school, early as it had happened, but she never did discover why she was summoned in the first place. Because by the time she'd recovered somewhat, Miss Carter was chafing her hands briskly as she half-sat, half-lay on a settee in the office and saying, 'I'll not make the usual snide comments about morning sickness because in your case I'm sure there's some other ...' She stopped abruptly as a flood of colour rose in Leonie's pale cheeks. 'My dear, I was only joking, I assure you . . .'

But to Leonie's horror, hot tears of distress and embarrassment welled and there seemed to be nothing she could do to stop them. On top of everything, she'd hardly slept for nights on end and to turn aside what Miss Carter had said in all innocence with the lightness it should have deserved, was suddenly impossible. In fact all she could do was bury her head in her hands and weep.

The head observed her critically for a moment then she turned aside and picked up her telehone and spoke quietly into it.

The result of her call proved to be a tray of tea and biscuits which she accepted at the door. And when Leonie had mastered herself sufficiently, she made her drink some of the hot sweet tea and eat a couple of the biscuits.

'Now,' she said gently then, 'if you *are* pregnant, Miss Powell, I'd very much like you to tell me about it so that,' she waved aside Leonie's visible flinching, 'so that I can *help*.'

Leone blinked, causing Miss Carter to smile ruefully. 'My dear,' she said, 'a headmistress I might have become, a teacher I've been for years but firstly and foremostly I'm a woman, too, and even although I'm a spinster, I'm very conscious of the burdens just being a woman places on us. In fact, it's one of my pet themes . . . I believe we should help each other. It's not anything wickedly unique to . . . love unwisely,' her eyes were very direct, 'if that is what's happened to you. But no man has to pay for it in the unique way a woman does. Which is why I think we should stick together ... Would you like to tell me about it?'

To her surprise, Leonie found herself doing just that. And right from the beginning, from Tom, although she omitted Guy Richardson's name or that it was anyone connected with the school. 'The irony of it,' she said unsteadily at the end, 'is that I've twice ... loved unwisely now, as you put it.'

'Well, that rather remains to be seen,' Miss Carter said thoughtfully. 'As for your husband, was that love?'

'I ... I thought so at the time,' she said unhappily. 'Now I don't know if this is just a different version of—of what is *not* love. That probably doesn't make any sense to you.'

Miss Carter smiled wisely. 'Miss Powell, if I thought I was an expert on what is and what is not love, my life might have taken a very different course. But, tell me, this man, the father of your baby, he's not married is he?'

'Oh no ...'

'Then why are you automatically assuming ...?'

'Because,' Leonie stood up restlessly, 'there are reasons why he might not have thought of marriage, sound reasons. But this—to the kind of man he is, might seem like a cast-iron reason to marry me. But because we've made a baby ... that's not proof that we love each other, is it? It ... it was an accident. Oh *damn*,' she said passionately, 'I'm so confused ...'

'And frightened,' Miss Carter said quietly. 'Of men. Frightened to love this man, to put yourself in that position again?'

'Yes,' Leonie whispered. 'Yes ... The last time we saw each other, he was angry with me over something I couldn't really help. I ... oh, it's been nothing like ... how it was with Tom but all the same ...'

'Is it *that* more than your fears that he might not wish to marry you?'

'I ... it's part of it,' Leonie said hoarsely and honestly. 'The other part is that I don't *really* know what he feels for me and now that this has happened, I might never know.'

'But they're one and the same thing, Miss Powell,' Miss Carter said after a while. 'A lack of trust, a lack of confidence ... in yourself. Confidence in your judgment.'

'I don't have a great record in that, my judgment.'

'Have you seen him recently?'

'I ... no. He's out of town at present.'

'Then may I make a suggestion? I have a cottage on the beach at Tugun. It's nothing grand but the beach is magnificent—unfortunately I don't spend as much time as I'd like to there but I've found it's a great place for restoring your spirits. Now I can arrange for you to have two weeks' sick leave and I think you should go there and really try to think this out in peace and solitude ...'

'But ... the music exams ...'

'My dear, we will manage. If you're going to suffer from nausea, you won't be able to work anyway. But this is a way of putting all the added complications like your job and so on, on ice so to speak. And a way for you to concentrate on the deeper issues. I think it's what you should do. And at the end of the time, come and see me and we'll talk again.' She reached into a drawer and produced a bunch of keys from which she extracted two. 'I'll write the address down. How are you placed for cash at the moment?'

'I'm fine,' Leonie said huskily and a little wonderingly. 'I don't know how to thank you . . .'

'There's nothing to thank me for. The place is empty.'

'All the same, you've been so very understanding . . .'

'Well I told you why earlier.' Mis Carter grimaced. 'But there's something else. I've been very impressed with you, Miss Powell, as a person who can handle girls firmly but humanly, as someone with quite considerable musical talent, but also just as someone I like . . .'

As it happened Leonie delayed her departure to Tugun by a day—it was only an hour's bus ride down the coast.

But the reason she delayed it was because on her way home from school that fateful morning, she saw Guy Richardson's silver Rolls Royce threading its way through the Southport traffic ahead of the bus. She couldn't make him out precisely, just a dark head behind the wheel but all the same her heart began to pound and she thought, Oh God, he's back . . . Will he come to see me?

By the end of the following day though, it was obvious he had no intention of doing that and the fact of it seemed to Leonie to be like a coffin nail to her secret hopes—that he would relent in this cold war first.

And when she tried to examine why it was so important to her that he did, she came to the conclusion that for her to be the one to relent, smacked to her of how she'd been with Tom—willing to take the blame for anything. Well, if not willing, doing it all the same, subduing her instincts which had told her she was not in the wrong, pretending . . . faking again in a way. Also, if Guy could take her or leave her so easily . . .

She brushed the tears from her eyes and the next morning she took the bus to Tugun, leaving behind a saddened and perplexed Spider.

'At least tell me where you're going, Leonie.'

'Spider,' she sighed and looked at him lovingly, 'the truth is, I've got myself into a bit of a mess. And if I told you where I was going, you might find it hard to . . . to lie to someone about it. Because I don't want anyone to know where I am. *If* . . . they should ask . . .'

'The man with the silver Rolls,' Spider said knowingly and added bitterly, 'I could kill him if he's hurt you!'

'Oh, Spider, it was my fault,' she said. 'But I want you to know that I'll keep in touch with you when this is all over. Because you've been so kind.'

Spider removed his glasses and wiped his faded blue eyes. 'Never had a daughter,' he said. 'But if I had, I'd have liked her to be like you. You *sure* this is the right way of going about things?'

'I'm sure,' she said unsteadily. 'And I've packed all my things in case I don't come back. So if I write and ask you to forward them for me, it will just be a matter of getting a carrier . . .'

It was a miserable trip down the coast and even the weather conspired against her—drizzling rain and a cold wind so that by the time she'd located Miss Carter's cottage, she was soaked, despite her umbrella, and half frozen and not the magnificent setting of the old-fashioned little fibro house a few steps up the green hill from the beach, nor the spectacle of angry waves and limitless heavy grey sky, had the power to restore her although she loved the sea in all its moods.

But today she could feel only bereft and alone and desperate. And ill ... And she went to bed after a cold shower because the hot water system took time to heat up after being switched on, more to try and warm herself than with any expectation of sleeping. Yet she did, deeply, to wake up after it was dark only to turn over and go to sleep again until the early morning.

CHAPTER NINE

Two days later, her desperation and misery had subsided from an acute, aching level to a duller less intense pain, yet something that was there all the time.

The weather improved but it was by now mid-winter and to a Queenslander born and bred, it was cold. So the beach, with its wide white sands that stretched to Coolangatta in the distance was all but deserted although the sun shone. And the rare hardy souls who did swim were surfies in wet suits or visitors from down south.

She walked a lot and found herself reading a lot from Miss Carter's comprehensive bookcase. And at other times she sat on the veranda and watched the sea.

The cottage was fully equipped with linen and kitchen utensils, but there was no television, no radio even. Only an old-fashioned record player but plenty of records to choose from of mainly light classical music. And once a day, Leonie walked up to the shopping centre of Tugun to buy supplies. Otherwise she spoke to no-one.

The one thing she didn't do was really think. It seemed her brain could absorb what she read, take pleasure in the music she played and the endlessly changing moods of the sea, but it could not get to grips with what she was really there for ... as if it had gone numb to any imput she herself had to contribute.

But finally, by the time she'd been there a week,

she was sitting on the veranda one evening after a simple meal of scrambled eggs on toast, rugged up against the chill of the night, when she found herself thinking of Guy with a clear, piercing intensity that made her catch her breath and wince at the pain it brought her. She could picture him in her mind's eye as if he was right there in front of her. The lines of his face that she knew so well now, the sometimes wickedly amused glint in his dark blue eyes, the lazy way he could look at her that made her pulses leap and her body quiver.

And she had to bite her lip to stop the tears from taking over. And she thought suddenly, Miss Carter is right, to run away from him proves nothing except that I'm running away from myself ... My scared, cowardly self that lacks any confidence or courage. If he's done nothing else, he's shown a willingness to communicate with me—even the reason we fell out was because he wanted to know what was wrong. Surely I can talk to him at least, discuss this, tell him of my fears. Surely I know him well enough to know that I *can* talk to him ...

She swallowed and clenched her fists so that her nails bit into her palms because although she knew it was what she should do, the same old uncertainties were there, not to be banished with a magic wand. Yet there seemed to be a well of resolve within her and she thought, I'll go back tomorrow ...

But she slept restlessly that night. And the next morning she packed her bag with unsteady hands and locked the cottage up but stood on the veranda for a long time before she turned away and walked down the stairs and towards the road.

Nor was her state of mind helped by the fact

that long, slow bus trips with dozens of stops between Tugun and Surfer's, taken relatively early in the morning appeared not to agree with pregnant ladies ... At least not this one, she thought, as half-way there she gave up the unequal struggle against an overpowering sense of queasiness and got off and started to walk until she felt better. Then she took a taxi, but even so by the time she arrived at Guy's building, she was feeling exhausted and then he wasn't in ...

She leant her forehead against his door and tried to think. And finally thought of Peggy a few floors down.

But Peggy wasn't home either, only Bob and he was just leaving himself, in fact locking the door behind him as she got out of the lift.

'Leonie!' he said, surprise written large on his face. 'I'm afraid Peggy's out but ...' He tailed off and looked at her queerly. 'Are you all right?'

'I ... Bob,' she twisted her hands awkwardly, 'yes, I'm all right. Actually I came to see Guy but he's not home. Is he ... away again on business?'

'No. No, he's not. He's ... well, I saw him last night!' He smiled at her but it seemed a little strained.

'Then he must be at work,' she murmured more to herself. 'Why didn't I think of that?'

'As a matter of fact,' Bob said and hesitated, 'er ... he's not. In fact he should be home quite soon. Why don't you wait for him?' He wrinkled his brow thoughtfully. 'Unfortunately I've got a meeting in ten minutes but you could—hang on, we've got a key to his unit! When he's away his cleaning lady who comes in regularly gets it from Peggy. Why don't I get it for you and you can wait for him up there!' He began to unlock the door.

'I don't . . .' Leonie started to say uncertainly but in that instant she knew she could go no further without embarrassing herself by being sick in public, and anyway Bob wasn't listening.

With the result that five minutes later she was in Guy's unit and Bob was saying anxiously, 'Now you just put your feet up, love. You really don't look too well . . . Darn it! I'm going to cancel my meeting!'

Leonie took a deep, deep breath. 'Bob, *no*,' she said. 'It's not anything serious, I promise you. I'll just do as you say, and wait for Guy.' She smiled palely.

'All right,' Bob said slowly. 'If you promise me that, too, that you'll wait for Guy.'

'I will . . .'

In fact, she didn't have long to wait. Just long enough to finally get rid of her breakfast and clean herself up. So that she looked almost normal, pale still, she saw in the bathroom mirror and with dark smudges beneath her eyes, but tidy. Then, just as she was collecting up her toothbrush and other gear to restore them to her bag, she heard the front door open and shut and she went still and felt her heart flutter in her breast. And she turned rather frantic eyes to the door and wished she could run, hide—something, but knew there was no escape. She had to go out and face him . . .

But the ordeal was tempered at first in a curious way. For Guy was standing leaning his head back against the front door with his eyes closed and his hands hanging limply by his sides, and his face pale, too, and set in frightening lines of suffering.

And he didn't hear her until she said convulsively, 'Guy? What is it? Is ... has something happened to Claire?'

His eyes flew open then and he straightened and looked for a moment as if he thought he was seeing things as they rested on her. Then they hardened and he said through his teeth, 'Not Claire, *you*. Don't you ever do that to me again, Leonie. If you're tired of me or you've found someone else, *tell* me for God's sake. I might be able to handle that. But not knowing ... I got two bloody speeding tickets on the way to Tugun this morning,' he said savagely. 'Not that I care but ...'

'Tugun ...' Her eyes were wide and confused. 'How did you know ...?'

'Not from your friend Spider,' he said bitterly.

'Then ...'

'Yes. Miss Carter. I went straight from him to her.'

'D-did ... did you ...' The words seemed to stick in her throat.

'I told her about us,' he said with a kind of white-lipped precision. 'All that *I* know about us, that is. Which is not a lot. I think I surprised her—in a way. But it was obvious, not altogether. Because all I could get out of her was where you were, not why you'd run away. Not your side of the story, just where you were. Only you weren't there any longer ...'

'Because,' she said shakily, 'I was on my way back here. Guy ... when did you get back from Darwin?'

'Last night,' he said briefly.

'But ... but ...' she stammered. 'I saw you a week ago in Southport.'

'You couldn't have ...'

'I did ... well I saw your car ...'

His eyes narrowed. 'It went in for an overhaul about a week ago. A mechanic picked it up from the garage here.'

'Oh ...' she breathed.

'And if you're wondering why I stayed away so long—the trip came up unexpectedly in the first place and then got extended but it was a chance to get the contract for new boats for the Northern Territory Water Police—whatever they call themselves——' he said impatiently, 'so I stayed on. But I wrote to you, in a sense.'

She licked her lips.

'I wrote to Claire, actually, explaining about us. And I asked her to tell you that I'd been delayed ... In fact I should still be up there but I got a letter back from Claire saying you weren't there to tell. They—the official story at school was that you'd been taken ill. It was a very happy letter ... As a matter of fact Claire said to me quite some time ago that if I ever thought of remarrying, she knew just the person for me. You ...'

Leonie swallowed. 'Claire ... said to me once that she thought it might be hard to share you with someone. Also ... that you would always love her mother ...'

'Claire is only twelve,' he said. 'And she's right, it would take some adjustments for her if I married again. But less than if she remembered her mother ... and with someone understanding and sensitive, someone she obviously likes, nothing insurmountable. What other doubts do you have about me, Leonie?' he added harshly.

She flinched. 'Guy ...'

'Do you want me to tell you how it happened for me? As a matter of fact it will be quite a relief—I've stopped myself from saying these things time and time again. But the plain truth is that I fell in love with you that first day ... Strange how these things happen, isn't it?' He smiled twistedly. 'A pair of eyes, *something* about you that I couldn't put my finger on ... that's all it took.'

'Oh, Guy,' she whispered, her eyes glittering with tears.

'But at the same time I began to realise that it wasn't going to be that simple. That something was a very real threat to it ever becoming a two-way thing. Do you remember when we had that barbecue on the beach?'

'Yes ...'

'You were right. I was thinking about Marie because I knew I'd fallen in love with you ... I was farewelling her finally, I guess. Then the next morning I was cursing myself because I was realising more and more that to have fallen in love with Leonie Powell was something I might one day regret ...'

Leonie lifted her hands to her face but he went on remorselessly in the same hard voice ... 'Not that I gave up hope. I don't think that happened until this morning ... Strangely enough I didn't even give up hope after you'd told me about your husband. In fact that gave me *renewed* hope. At least I knew what I was dealing with. Someone who'd been hurt, disillusioned and was understandably wary of men. Why do you think I let you go? I knew it was no good trying to force you into anything, I knew you'd take fright and that I could destroy anything that might have existed for you and me ... I thought, I'll give her plenty of breathing space and time. But all the same I enlisted Peggy's aid. I asked her to get in touch with you, to try and draw you into her circle of friends where we might meet again. She didn't take much persuading ... All the same, wondering whether you'd let her was like a nightmare. Then I saw you at that party ... Leonie, look at me.'

'I can't,' she said hoarsely into her hands.

'I saw you at the party,' he went on in a lower voice, 'and what happened ... happened. And I thought, I thought I'm on the home stretch now. At least she trusts me. But out of the blue,' he took her wrists and drew her hands from her face and she stared up at him wordlessly, 'at the musical, you were afraid of me again for some reason and you made it quite obvious you didn't trust me at all. I know ... I know the circumstances were ... crazy, Leonie, and if only we'd had more time before that bloody musical I wouldn't have let it happen like that. But it was *more* than that, I could tell. And it came like a blow to me. So much so I got angry and said what I did ... Because you see,' his lips were barely moving and his eyes darker than midnight, 'I once said something to you that I've since disproved entirely to myself. You *can* love someone deeply and desperately and bitterly and so that the pain never seems to go away—whether they love you in return or not.'

Her lips were trembling so much she couldn't speak. Instead, she bent her head and kissed his fingers that were around her wrist, kissed them yearningly and tenderly.

He stood perfectly still for a time, breathing as if he'd been running. Then he cupped her cheek with his other hand and said her name hoarsely as if it had been torn out of him. 'Leonie ... will you tell me why you ran away now?'

She raised her head. 'Yes, Guy,' she whispered. 'Because I'm a fool. I don't deserve ... all the things you've just told me.'

'Don't, oh God, don't,' he said and released her wrist to draw her into his arms. 'You're not.'

'Yes, I am,' she said against his shoulder. 'But it came as such a shock, you see. And, well, you did say yourself that we hadn't had much time. Also,' her voice cracked a little, 'I didn't know ... I mean I wondered whether you meant for us to be ... for me to be your mistress, for us to be like Laurel and Brad because of Claire, because of Marie.' She swallowed as he tensed but didn't look away. And she said to the look in his eyes, 'I'm sorry, so sorry ...'

'I would have cleared that up a lot earlier,' he said finally, 'only I didn't think you were ready to hear it. But what came as such a shock?'

She bit her lip, still a little afraid in her heart to tell him. And suddenly his eyes narrowed and he frowned and held her away from him and looked her up and down intently then let his eyes rest on her pale, weary face and the dark smudges beneath her eyes.

And he said slowly, 'Taken ill ... Oh my darling, how could I have been so blind? Are we,' he touched her face with unsteady fingers, 'are we going to have a baby?'

She couldn't help smiling through her tears. 'Don't you mind?'

'If you don't ... Why should I mind? When— the very first time?'

She nodded. 'Well, the first or second time ...'

'I bet it was the first,' he said softly.

'How can you be sure?'

'I can feel it in my bones. It was so special.'

'It was for me, too . . .' But she moved in his arms. 'There are problems, though. Claire might be only twelve but I'm sure she can count.'

'Leonie . . .' His voice was suddenly different and very direct.

She interrupted him though to say with difficulty, 'And it's . . . well more competition for her, too.'

'As a matter of fact Claire is crazy about babies. She dotes on them. But,' he waited until she stilled and looked up into his eyes, 'if we love each other, and we love Claire, we'll find a way round any problems, believe me.'

'I . . . was so afraid to tell you,' she said after a long time and laid her cheek in the opening of his shirt.

'Will you promise me one thing? From now on, trust me.'

'Oh, Guy,' she whispered, 'I do now. And I love you and I need you more than you'll ever know. And I'm so grateful to you . . .'

'Hey,' he said and picked her up in his arms, 'that's my line.'

'No, it's not . . .'

'Perhaps we better settle for a compromise.' His dark blue eyes glinted suddenly.

'Oh?'

'Mmm,' he said and sat down with her in his lap. 'Like a change of subject. How about this?' And he bent his head and kissed her.

Quite a bit later, she said a little indistinctly, 'Is that what you call a change of subject?' He'd opened the front of the tracksuit top she wore and the blouse beneath it and was touching her breasts tenderly.

'This?' He lifted his head and grinned at her but

the rest of what he was about to say was cut off by the ringing of the telephone. 'Hell,' he said instead, 'let it ring . . .'

Which it did then stopped only to start again within two minutes. He swore more explicitly then reluctantly lifted her off his lap and laid her in the corner of the settee, and went to answer it impatiently.

'Yes? Oh, Peggy . . . what's that? Yes, she's here . . . Bob was worried?' Leonie sat up as he turned to her but he only grimaced and said into the 'phone, 'As a matter of fact I hadn't got around to asking her how she got in, I was so relieved to see her . . . Well, there's a good reason for that so you can set Bob's mind at rest. How do you two fancy becoming godparents . . . in about seven-and-a-half months time, that is . . .' He listened patiently for a while and with a growing smile on his face. Then he said, 'Dear Peggy, of course I'm going to marry her first . . . Thanks, love, I'll tell her. In fact, thank you for everything, and Bob.'

He put the 'phone down and came back to her. 'You had us all worried.'

'They're very sweet,' she murmured.

'Yes . . . Where were we? What have you done?' He eyed her frowningly.

'Nothing,' she replied innocently but she'd pulled her blouse together.

'Don't mothers-to-be indulge in that kind of thing?' he asked gravely but with a smile at the back of his eyes as he took her loosely into his arms.

'Oh, I think they do . . . They just don't like to flaunt themselves.' She looked downwards fleetingly, her breath coming a little unevenly but he tipped her chin up with his fingers.

'Do you know,' he said unsteadily, 'what the thought of that does to me?'

She smiled mistily. 'No. Tell me . . .'

'I know of a better way than mere words.' But a look of concern crossed his face suddenly. 'How do you feel? If you don't feel up to . . .'

She cut his words off with a hand to his lips. 'I feel,' she said softly, 'relaxed, warm, safe—and for the moment, not sick—and just about to die of loving you and wanting you so much. That's how I feel.'

He stared down at her at last calm, loving eyes for a long time. Then a great sigh seemed to rack his body and he said huskily, 'Thank you, my love . . .' And he pulled her very close and kissed her deeply.

CHAPTER TEN

'PHILLIP!' Claire said. 'If you do that again I shall be very cross with you.'

Master Phillip Richardson, being not quite fifteen months and not yet a fast talker but very much alive to vocal nuances, beamed at his half-sister for her reproof had been delivered in such loving tones, he thought he was being praised.

'What's he doing?' Leonie enquired over her shoulder as she placed a casserole in the oven.

'Blowing bubbles with his food. And ... oh! Rubbing it in his hair!' Claire said exasperatedly. 'I'll have to give him a bath after this!'

'He's had enough,' Leonie said from experience and with a smothered grin. 'Listen, love, I've put your dinner in the oven. Tell Mrs Watson there's plenty for her, too, if she's hungry. And he had a bath not long ago. Perhaps . . .'

'Oh, I don't mind,' Claire said. 'And he really enjoys my baths. What time are you leaving? And where's Daddy taking you?'

'By rights I should be gone already and I don't know where he's taking me. He was rather mysterious about it.'

'It will be somewhere good then,' Claire said confidently. 'When he's in a mysterious mood it always is. Do you know, Leonie,' she added reflectively as she picked Phillip up out of his high chair, 'I never dreamt what I was missing out on, not having a family. It's been wonderful!' Her dark eyes glowed with sincerity.

'I'm so glad to hear you say that, darling,' Leonie replied with a sudden lump in her throat. 'And it has been for me, too. I . . . oh, there's Mrs Watson and I'm not even changed yet. Now she's sleeping over in case we're late. As for you . . .' someone particularly perceptive would have noticed the faintest sheen of tears in her eyes as she looked at her baby son and stepdaughter, their dark heads close, 'you grubby *little* darling, be good!' And she kissed them both.

'Oh, he's always good for me,' Claire replied placidly, conveniently forgetting why she was going to bath him again.

He is, too, Leonie thought as she slid into her car after a hasty shower and change. Well, she grinned to herself, he adores Claire. In fact, she mused as she drove from Runaway Bay into Surfer's, it's all turned out so well I sometimes feel like pinching myself . . .

Not long after their marriage, they'd bought a house not far from the marina and removed Claire from boarding school, although she still went to St Bede's as a day scholar. And although there'd been times when it hadn't been easy for any of them, patience had won the day and Phillip had really cemented the relationship. As Guy had predicted, Claire had been entranced from the moment she'd laid eyes on him.

Then, once Phillip had been weaned, Guy had asked Leonie idly if she'd like to go back to work, part-time. 'I ran into Miss Carter the other day. She asked after you, naturally, and said to tell you that they'd decided to form a school orchestra and asked if you'd be interested in running it say— three afternoons a week?'

Leonie caught her breath. 'I'd love it,' she said

candidly after a moment. 'But ... would you mind? And what about ...'

He grinned. 'Between you and Claire, that baby gets enough loving attention for six of them. And why should I mind? So long as *I* don't miss out on any tender loving care ...'

'You,' she answered, '... also get enough of that for six!'

But I wonder why he wouldn't tell me where we're going tonight? she thought with a smile curving her lips as she parked her car in the garage of the building where Guy still maintained the unit. She often used this place to park, when she came in shopping or to meet him. And sometimes they entertained in the unit or lent it to their friends from up country. Guy had plenty of those she'd discovered and they'd become her friends, too.

In fact, she was to meet him there tonight. Which is just as well, she thought, seeing as I'm running so late! Perhaps he's organised a group of us to go out to dinner and we're all meeting there ...

But when she opened the door on the twentieth floor with her own key, it was to see the lamps switched on and the curtains drawn but no-one there.

'Guy!' she called, 'I'm sorry I'm late but ... oh!' She jumped as she turned back from closing the door to find her husband directly behind her wearing only a bath towel around his waist. 'Oh, you frightened the life out of me ... but you're not even ready! And here I've been rushing like a mad thing.'

'I'm ready,' he said taking her in his arms and kissing her leisurely. 'Well, almost ...'

'Ready for *what?*' she asked laughingly and breathlessly when he'd finished.

His dark blue eyes glinted with little points of devilry. 'You,' he said simply.

'But . . . I mean, I'm flattered but . . .'

'Then you've forgotten,' he said in falsely tragic tones although his eyes still laughed at her.

'What?'

'It's our second anniversary . . .'

'Guy, it isn't. That's about three months away!'

'Not our wedding anniversary, sweetheart. It's the anniversary of the first time we made love.'

'I . . . oh . . . is it?'

'Give or take a few days. It's the same month,' he said gravely and released her to take her hand. 'Which to my mind is ample reason for a celebration . . . like this.'

He led her into the den where similar cartons from the Indonesian restaurant downstairs were set out on a table as they had been two years ago—give or take some weeks. And on the video machine was the tape of *The Sound of Music* . . .

'Oh, Guy,' she said with a break in her voice and tears in her eyes.

'I couldn't get *Oliver* but this was your second choice, wasn't it?'

She nodded wordlessly and lifted his hand to her mouth. 'I love you so much,' she whispered.

'Then you didn't mind not going out tonight?' he murmured much later.

'What do you think?' she answered with a smile trembling on her lips.

He lifted his head to rest it on one hand and let his gaze roam down the length of her as she lay beside him, her body gilded in the lamplight and still sprawled with a kind of voluptuous abandon as if she'd not had the strength to move after his lovemaking, nor wanted to.

They were lying on the same bed they'd used the first time they'd made love, but there were some subtle changes in her body since then. Her breasts were fuller and deeper and her nipples darker but these symbols of motherhood seemed to please him.

'I think,' he said slowly, 'that I can never find the words to tell you how much I love *you*.'

'I don't need you to tell me. Every day you show me in some way ... like tonight. It was perfect.'

He slid his hand into her hair. 'Do you want to go home?'

She considered for a moment. Then she said, 'No ... Let's make it a full night. Or is that wicked and sinful for an old married couple like we are? With two children?'

'Yes. Deliciously so ...' A smile lurked at the back of his eyes.

'But perhaps I should ring Mrs Watson. She is sleeping over but ...'

'I wouldn't bother.'

'Well, all the same ... but she'll be asleep now for sure.' Her eyes were slightly anxious.

'Like all good babysitters,' he said wryly. 'Actually I rang her myself earlier. You'd already left. I told her we wouldn't be home until lunchtime. She engaged to get Claire off to school on time and assured me Phillip would be fine with her. Phillip,' he added darkly, 'has a way with women obviously.'

'I wonder who he inherited that from?' Leonie replied innocently and added, 'I see! What would you have done if I'd wanted to go home now?'

'Kept you here by force. And had my way with you.'

'Again?'

'And again . . . why are you laughing?'

'I seem to be such a willing captive,' she said, her eyes adoring him. But after a moment they became tinged with confusion. 'I . . . never believed it could be like this. I keep wanting to pinch myself,' she said huskily.

'Do you think I didn't know that?'

She was silent.

'Leonie?'

'Mmm?'

'Believe it, my love,' he said softly and put his arms around her. 'It's here to stay.'

'I . . . promised you something once,' she said a little diffidently. 'You once ended a perfect day for me in a perfect way. This has been another perfect day . . . and it's my turn now. Don't move,' she whispered and began to caress his body slowly with her lips and her hands until with a muffled groan he caught her up in his arms again.

'You're not supposed to do that,' she teased.

'Then you shouldn't entice me to, my wicked, wanton wife,' he retorted and they came together with love, and laughter and joy.

And finally she whispered radiantly, 'I do believe it. I do . . .'

Harlequin Presents

Coming Next Month

895 STORM Vanessa Grant
After being stranded by a fierce storm in the Queen Charlotte Islands a reporter doubts herself, the hard-hitting pilot she desires and her commitment to a childhood sweetheart.

896 LOSER TAKE ALL Rosemary Hammond
A wealthy American doesn't exactly win his new bride in a poker game. But it amounts to the same thing, because it's marriage for them—win or lose!

897 THE HARD MAN Penny Jordan
Desire for a virtual stranger reminds a young widow and mother she is still a woman capable of love, capable of repeating the mistake she made ten years ago.

898 EXPLOSIVE MEETING Charlotte Lamb
A lab technician's boss resents his employee's impassioned plea on behalf of a brilliant scientist who keeps blowing up the lab. And he misinterprets her persistence—in more ways than one!

899 AN ALL-CONSUMING PASSION Anne Mather
When her father's right-hand man comes to the Caribbean to escort the boss's daughter back to London, she tries to make him forget his responsibilities—never thinking she is playing with fire.

900 LEAVING HOME Leigh Michaels
A young woman never dreams her guardian's decision to remain single had anything to do with her, until he proposes marriage—to pull her out of yet another scrape.

901 SUNSTROKE Elizabeth Oldfield
Can a widow reconcile receiving twenty thousand pounds to pay off her late husband's creditors with leaving the man she loves—even though he's been groomed to marry someone else?

902 DANGEROUS MOONLIGHT Kay Thorpe
It is possible that the Greek hotel owner a vacationer encounters isn't the same man who ruined her sister's marriage. But can she risk asking him outright, when the truth could break her heart?

Available in July wherever paperback books are sold, or through Harlequin Reader Service.

In the U.S.
901 Fuhrmann Blvd.
P.O. Box 1397
Buffalo, N.Y. 14240-1397

In Canada
P.O. Box 2800, Postal Station A
5170 Yonge Street
Willowdale, Ontario M2N 6J3

Can you keep a secret?

You can keep this one plus 4 free novels

WORLDWIDE LIBRARY IS YOUR TICKET TO ROMANCE, ADVENTURE AND EXCITEMENT

Experience it all in these big, bold Bestsellers— Yours exclusively from WORLDWIDE LIBRARY WHILE QUANTITIES LAST

To receive these Bestsellers, complete the order form, detach and send together with your check or money order (include 75¢ postage and handling), payable to WORLDWIDE LIBRARY, to:

In the U.S.
WORLDWIDE LIBRARY
901 Fuhrmann Blvd.
Buffalo, N.Y. 14269

In Canada
WORLDWIDE LIBRARY
P.O. Box 2800, 5170 Yonge Street
Postal Station A, Willowdale, Ontario
M2N 6J3

Quant.	Title	Price
_____	WILD CONCERTO, Anne Mather	$2.95
_____	A VIOLATION, Charlotte Lamb	$3.50
_____	SECRETS, Sheila Holland	$3.50
_____	SWEET MEMORIES, LaVyrle Spencer	$3.50
_____	FLORA, Anne Weale	$3.50
_____	SUMMER'S AWAKENING, Anne Weale	$3.50
_____	FINGER PRINTS, Barbara Delinsky	$3.50
_____	DREAMWEAVER,	
_____	Felicia Gallant/Rebecca Flanders	$3.50
_____	EYE OF THE STORM, Maura Seger	$3.50
_____	HIDDEN IN THE FLAME, Anne Mather	$3.50
_____	ECHO OF THUNDER, Maura Seger	$3.95
_____	DREAM OF DARKNESS, Jocelyn Haley	$3.95

	YOUR ORDER TOTAL	$_____
	New York and Arizona residents add appropriate sales tax	$_____
	Postage and Handling	$___.75
	I enclose	$_____

NAME _____

ADDRESS _____ APT.# _____

CITY _____

STATE/PROV. _____ ZIP/POSTAL CODE _____

WW-1-3